K. SEAN HARRIS

The Stud II

The saga continues…

Cover concept: *K. Sean Harris*
Cover Design: *Sanya Dockery*
Typeset & Book layout: *Sanya Dockery*

Published by: Book Fetish

Printed in the U.S.A   ISBN: 978-976-95303-1-7

And why wilt thou, my son, be ravished with a strange woman, and embrace the bosom of a stranger?

Proverbs 5:20

Let not him that is deceived trust in vanity: for vanity shall be his recompence.

Job 15:31

CHAPTER 1

Jerome opened his eyes and reached over to retrieve his cell phone from the bedside table and silenced the alarm. It was 6 a.m. Way too early to be up after a torrid threesome with two girls he had met at a cocktail party last night that he was invited to by the head of the Jamaica Football Association. He almost didn't go but was happy that he did. How often did a man get to have a ménage a tois with twins? They were the twenty year old daughters of the newly appointed German ambassador to Jamaica and huge football fans who were thoroughly impressed at Jerome's stature as the most popular football player in the Caribbean.

Jerome had almost peed his pants in excitement when after chatting with them for several minutes by the poolside; the outspoken one had boldly asked if he could manage her and her sister at the same time. He had slipped away with the girls and taken them to his apartment where he proceeded to show them just how well he could handle the two of them.

He smiled as he threw the covers aside and got out of bed. It had been a memorable night. He padded to the bathroom, urinated, brushed his teeth and washed his face. He then got dressed in sweats, a jersey and sneakers, and went into the kitchen to make his protein shake.

Ten minutes later he was out the door. He jogged over to Emancipation Park which was five minutes away from his apartment and did some stretches as he prepared to do calisthenics and several laps around the park. He had to report to Manchester FC in four and a half weeks to start training for the up coming season and he planned to be in the best shape of his life.

Angela woke up at 7:30 and quickly got ready to go to work. Today was going to be a long one. Six clients, with the last, a cricketer for the West Indies team who was back home in Jamaica rehabbing after injuring his back during a recent Test match in Pakistan, would be coming at 5:30 for a two hour session. She sent Jerome a text while she had a quick breakfast of frosted flakes and a bagel with cream cheese and orange juice.

She loved him so much. After her heartbreaking experience with her ex, Jerome had shown her in the short month that they were together, the true meaning of happiness. And it would only get better. At twenty-two he was two years younger than her but it didn't matter. He was mature, accomplished and on his way to greater things. Handsome, sexy, and blessed with a dick that was too big and sweet to be true. And he loved her. What more could a woman want?

She got a response from him as she pulled up in the parking lot of her business place.

Hey sugar bun. How's my baby doing this morning? Got in late from the function last night but out exercising now. Gotta get in tip top shape! I love you. Call me when you take your lunch break. xoxoxo

Angela smiled as she answered his text. Jerome was already in great shape. His body was like a well oiled machine. But she admired his dedication to his craft. He was about to take it to a whole other level when he goes to England to play for one of the top teams in the world's most competitive football league. She was confident that he would excel. Jerome was a special talent. And he was driven. An unbeatable combination.

She had no idea how she was going to deal with being away from him for months on end. It was going to be very difficult. She and her family – well her dad anyway, in case Sara didn't want to come and her mom had to stay back with her - would be at his first game to start the season but she would only be in London for a week. She couldn't stay away from her practice longer than that. Her assistant, Suzzette, was already having a warm time rearranging her schedule to accommodate the trip.

She tossed the phone into her pocketbook after sending the message and exited the car. Her first patient was her favourite. Little Adrian. Such a sweet boy. Despite enduring a bad spinal injury in a horrible car accident, two corrective surgeries and having to go through extensive physiotherapy, he was the most cheerful nine year old that she had ever met.

Helping him on his journey to walk again was a great way to start the day.

Lenky woke up with a hard on. It was about time. He hadn't been horny since his brother died. He couldn't tell the last time that he had gone ten days without sex. He looked over at his wife. Laura was still dead to the world. Waking up early was not her cup of tea. He reached down and stroked his dick as he slowly pulled the covers from off of them. She was wearing a Donna Karan night shirt. Her firm breasts jutted provocatively against the sheer black fabric. She was lying on her side, her large, round ass partially exposed. Blood surged to his center. He was now harder than a Roman column. Laura might get pissed if he woke her up but he didn't care. He needed some. Now. He got behind her and slid down. He gently raised one of her legs and ran his tongue along the slit of her shaven mound like a swipe card. She stirred at first; then woke up when he stuck his tongue inside her.

"Baby...what are you doing...mmmm..." she murmured sleepily, her eyes half-open. It was the first time that he was having sex with her since Mikey's death a week and a half ago, so though she was annoyed, she didn't protest.

Lenky swung her leg over in response and climbed on top of her. He was pleased to see that she was already wet. She wanted him. He slid his dick inside her and groaned at the always pleasurable feel of her hot depths. They say that pregnant pussy is the sweetest pussy and Lenky was not about to disagree. Her pussy felt so good. He felt like he was floating. He climaxed even quicker than his customary five minutes. Ten strokes were all he could muster before he spilled his seed inside her with a loud roar.

He rolled over onto his back and laid there breathing heavily as Laura got up and went inside the bathroom to clean up.

She sat on the toilet and sighed as she wiped his semen before it ran down her legs. Damn Lenky for interrupting her dream for one minute of sex. She was dreaming that Jerome had her spread-eagled on the floor in his living room, pounding her into ecstasy, when he had woken her up. That's why she was already so wet. Asshole. He messed up her orgasm in her dream and didn't even have the decency to give her one in real life. Lenky rarely ever made her climax. Matter of fact, in the twenty months that they had been together, she could only remember having an orgasm three times. Jerome could give her more than that in one session. When she last had sex with him four days ago she had climaxed so many times that she lost count.

Laura sighed and shrugged off her nightshirt.

She decided to go and help herself in the shower before going back to bed.

CHAPTER 2

Lenky was thoughtful as he took a deep drag off the huge marijuana joint that Blacka had just rolled for him. He had just eaten breakfast prepared by Blacka, who was a decent cook, and who had been handling the cooking around the house since Bigga, the former chef, was killed a few weeks ago. A new chef would be hired soon but with Mikey's death, Lenky had not yet gotten around to hiring one. Food was the last thing on his mind these days.

He exhaled and opened the door to Mikey's room. He went inside and closed the door behind him. He had instructed the cleaning lady not to go in there so everything was as Mikey had left it. Tears welled up in Lenky' eyes as he looked around the messy room. Clothes were strewn on the bed and the carpeted floor, a half-smoked joint was in the ashtray, never to be picked up again by its owner; and an empty condom wrapper was on the dresser.

Lenky sat on the edge of the bed and cried like a baby. Mikey was a pain in the ass most of the time but he really loved his little brother. It had just been the two of them. Their mother had passed away twelve years ago and they never had a relationship with their father and his side of the family. He had practically raised Mikey on his own.

He knew that he needed to pull himself together. Business was suffering a bit from his lack of attention and there were some important decisions to be made but he would get back on track after the funeral.

Right now he just needed to grieve.

Michelle watched as they began to shoot the bedroom scene. She was on the set of the music video for Cheetah's official first single. Cheetah was Jamaica's latest singing sensation. She was discovered at a wedding where she sang for the bride and groom. The bride's brother was one of Jamaica's notable up and coming producers and he immediately approached her to work with him. The results were spectacular so far. Cheetah's introduction to the public, a reggae remake of Toni Braxton's *Breathe Again*, shot straight to number one on the local charts and her collaboration with Jah Fever, an established reggae singer, was doing very well in Europe, having charted in Italy and France.

Michelle was the make-up artist commissioned to do everyone participating in the shoot and she was pleased with her handiwork. Cheetah was looking beautiful. It felt good being back on the job. After the fight with Laura, her self-esteem, along with her face, had taken a battering. Both were now very much on the mend, and she was feeling and looking great again. She had not left the house without her pepper spray. She wasn't sure if Laura would try to attack her again but if she did, she vowed to be ready this time. It certainly would not go down like it did before.

"Cut!" the director yelled.

Michelle went over to Cheetah to touch up her make-up. She couldn't wait for the shoot to end. She was supposed to be meeting up with Jerome afterwards.

Her pussy seeped moisture at the thought.

"I'm hungry," Laura announced, eyeing the Burgers & More sign a few meters ahead at the plaza on the left. "I'm going to be as big as a cow if I keep this up during my entire pregnancy. I ate just before I left the house an hour ago."

Khianna laughed. She knew what it was like. When she was pregnant with Malik, her three year old son, she had eaten round the clock like food was going out of style. But she had lost all the weight after her pregnancy and now you couldn't tell by looking at her that she had a child.

Laura turned into the plaza and parked in a spot in front of the fast food restaurant that had just been vacated by a Dodge Ram. They exited the vehicle and went inside. A pretty Indian girl passed them on their way in and Khianna thought of Michelle. She knew about the beef between her and Laura but when Laura had called her saying that if she still wanted to hang out with her she couldn't be friends with Michelle any more, she made her choice. Michelle was cool and all but Laura was also cool and rich. A no-brainer in her book.

They ordered and went to a window table over on the far right. Laura sighed as she bit into her bacon cheeseburger deluxe. She wished that she could confide in Khianna about the situation of not being sure who the father of her baby is. Khianna was cool to hang out with but she couldn't trust her the way she could Michelle. But what to do? Michelle was history. She had committed the cardinal sin by fucking her man, regardless of the fact that she had a husband. She had broken the code. There was no excuse.

Laura checked the time. It was now 3 p.m. After eating they would hit the mall and try to find her a dress to wear to Mikey's funeral on Sunday. She had tons of dresses in her closet to choose from but she wanted something new. She also needed to get a new suit for Lenky and also a suit for Mikey to be buried in. Lenky was in no shape to be dealing with funeral arrangements. Everything rested on her shoulders.

Soon it would be all over and her life back to normal. Well as normal as it could be being pregnant with the possibility of the baby's father being her husband's best friend. She wondered what Jerome was doing.

She retrieved her cell phone from her Coach tote bag and dialed his number.

Jerome swung by the upscale mansion where the video shoot that Michelle was working at was taking place. He had called when he was through at the manicurist and she had told him that they were almost done for the day. He parked and went inside, nodding a greeting to the people milling about and shaking a few hands. When he got to the room where they were shooting, Michelle and Cheetah were sitting on the bed laughing about something, while the camera crew packed up their equipment.

"Hi Jerome," Michelle gushed, jumping up to give him a hug.

"Is he your boyfriend?" Cheetah queried, looking at Jerome appraisingly.

"No, we're just good friends," Michelle answered slowly, almost reluctantly, suddenly regretting not meeting Jerome outside. Cheetah was looking at him like he was a delicious piece of meat.

Cheetah, clad in a black and gold Dolce & Gabbana two piece, got up and introduced herself.

"I'm Cheetah," she said, ignoring his outstretched hand and giving him a hug. She hugged him close, and Jerome's manicured paws cupped her ass cheeks casually like they belonged to him.

Though she knew that she had no claims on him, Michelle felt a pang of jealousy.

"Hi Jerome!" an excited voice said from the doorway. A pretty extra that was playing the 'other girl' in the video came into the room with a camera and asked if she could have a picture with him. Jerome obliged and also signed her shorts.

"Ah, you're that football star," Cheetah commented, looking at Jerome thoughtfully. "I thought you looked familiar."

Jerome merely flashed the smile that had dropped hundreds of draws in three continents as he looked her over. Cheetah was hot. Flawless skin, long legs that didn't seem to end, flat stomach highlighted by a rose gold navel ring, small perky breasts, high cheekbones and piercing eyes. She was on Laura's level, just a way more petite version. And she could sing her ass off. He wouldn't mind helping her to hit some high notes.

"Bye Cheetah," Michelle said, ready to go. "See you tomorrow."

"Ok Mich," Cheetah replied, her eyes still on Jerome.

Jerome nodded goodbye to her, giving her a lingering gaze, then he and Michelle made their way outside.

They climbed into Lenky's black Lexus SUV that he had loaned Jerome to use whenever he wanted, and headed down the winding driveway.

"Hungry?" Jerome asked, glancing at her.

Michelle sighed and tried to shrug away her irritation at the byplay that had occurred between Jerome and Cheetah.

"Yeah," Michelle replied, smiling at him. "For your dick."

Jerome laughed and headed towards her apartment to feed her.

CHAPTER 3

Michelle looked back at Jerome, her pretty face an intricate blend of pain, pleasure and disbelief, not necessarily in that order. Jerome was behind her, stroking her like only he could, his massive sugar-coated tool navigating the hot, turbulent waters of her extremely wet pussy, finding her pleasure points with ease and precision like it had a built-in compass. She was getting ready to come again. For the fourth time. She felt like she was going to pass out. And it was like this every single time that they had sex.

She was trying her hardest not to fall in love with Jerome but her efforts were futile. He was too handsome, too sweet, too exciting and too charming. Plus he fucked like he invented sex. She didn't stand a chance. Now that a little time had passed, she now understood – didn't forgive her – but she understood how Laura, despite being married, could lose her mind and fight her over Jerome. The man was unreal. He was also a dog. But God what a pedigree.

"Tell me how my dick feels," Jerome commanded, smacking her left ass cheek as he went harder, deeper.

"It feels so good Jerome...Jesus...too good..." Michelle whimpered, her orgasm now rapidly approaching.

Jerome was impossibly deep now, plunging relentlessly, like he wanted to exit through her mouth.

"Jerome...mmmmm...hurts...oh god...hurts so good ...coming...coming again Jerome...fuck...yes...yes... yesssssssssss!"

Michelle shook violently as she climaxed hard, feeling like she had an orgasm in her brain simultaneously with her pussy.

Jerome wasn't far behind. He groaned loudly as he filled her with his hot seed, bucking like a bronco.

The flood of his hot semen prolonged Michelle's orgasm, and their bodies trembled in unison.

"Enjoy your dinner baby?" Jada asked, hugging Lenky from behind. She was worried about him. Since Mikey's death he was a shadow of his former self. He was very quiet, barely eating and he hadn't fucked her in almost two weeks. She was extremely jealous of Laura being pregnant and was hoping fervently that it wouldn't be a girl. Lenky loved the son that she had given him but she knew that he badly wanted a little girl. And she wanted to be the one to give it to him. She hated Laura so much. The gold-digging bitch had come out of nowhere and snatched her man away. She was the one that had laid the ground-work, had been there before Lenky was rich, stuck with him through thick and thin, yet Laura was the one with the ring after only being on the scene for little over a year. Life was so unfair. But she loved him and she wasn't going to give up. One day she was going to reclaim her rightful spot. Time was the master of everything.

"Yeah," Lenky replied, though his plate of dumplings, boiled plantain and stew chicken was still half-full. He looked over at Nathaniel who was on the floor in front of the T.V. playing video games as usual.

He retrieved a dime bag of marijuana from his shirt pocket and proceeded to roll himself a joint while Jada cleared the table. She returned from the kitchen with an ice cold bottle of Guiness and handed it to him. He took a long swig and then lit his joint, inhaling deeply.

"Let's go inside the bedroom baby," Jada cooed, hoping that the weed and alcohol would help to get him in the mood. She couldn't very well get pregnant for him if he wasn't fucking her now could she? Lenky got up from the table and followed her to the bedroom.

Jada closed the door behind them.

"I'm so tired baby," Angela said through a yawn as she snuggled up next to Jerome under the covers. "But I still want some..."

"I've created an animal," Jerome teased, looking over at his vibrating cell phone on the right bedside table. He reached for it and looked at the caller ID. It was a UK number. He answered it.

"Hello," he said, sighing contentedly as Angela covered his right nipple with her hot mouth.

"What's up mate...its Brixton's finest."

Jerome laughed. Gunner. It was good to hear from him.

He tried to stifle a groan. Angela was now covering his stomach with soft, fluttery kisses.

"I'm here chilling with wifey. Everything good?" Jerome asked.

"Yeah, just getting in from a party innit. I'm coming to Jamaica next week Tuesday."

Jerome squirmed as Angela ran her velvety tongue along his defined abs. He was pleased that Gunner would be coming after Mikey's funeral. He was going to be spending a lot of time with Gunner for the duration of his visit and show him a good time, same as Gunner did for him when he had visited the UK; and Lenky would have been extra jealous of that, especially seeing as he was getting ready to bury his brother. Lenky was already jealous of the fact that he and Gunner had become such good friends in such a short space of time. Gunner's trip was going to be interesting to say the least.

17

"Wicked, good to hear that. We have a lot to catch up on but let me call you back tomorrow," Jerome told him, his breathing becoming laboured as Angela licked his scrotum and stroked his now tumescent dick.

Gunner laughed, guessing that Jerome was getting some action.

"Do your thing playboy, catch you later yeah," Gunner told him and terminated the call.

"Mmmmmm...damn baby...mmmmm..." Jerome moaned. He put the phone down and ran his fingers through Angela's silky mane as she pursed her lips and concentrated on the head of his dick.

"I need you inside me baby...need you to fill me up..." she told him as she rose and climbed on top of him.

"Take it baby...it's yours..." Jerome moaned, caressing her firm breasts and pinching her large nipples gently as she guided his dick inside her tight wetness.

"Ohhhhh...sweet Jesus...mmmm...yes Lord..." Angela groaned as she slid down his lengthy pole ever so gently. "Big ass dick...goddamn...mmmmm..."

"You don't love it? Huh? You don't love your dick?" Jerome asked, gripping her ass cheeks firmly as he forced her all the way down and back up again, over and over.

"Oh god! Yes! I love it baby! I fucking love it! Sweetest dick in the world!" Angela croaked as she bounced up and down his shaft, savouring its rigid sweetness, feeling her orgasm rushing to her center impatiently. It never ceased to amaze her how easily Jerome could make her climax. It was like he had designed her pussy.

He timed her orgasm perfectly and pinched her nipples as she climaxed. She howled from the intricate mix of pain and pleasure as she showered his dick with her juices.

"Baby...oh baby...Jesus Christ...ohhhhh..." she whimpered as she slumped on his chest, still shivering from the aftershocks.

After a few moments, still deeply embedded inside her, Jerome turned them sideways and resumed stoking her fire. He lifted her left leg for better access and gave her deep, lengthy strokes, eliciting strange sounds from her pussy and unfeminine grunts from her mouth.

She could feel his dick pulsing. He was going to climax soon. She wondered if he was going to make her come again before he did. Using his left arm to brace her left leg high in the air, Jerome climbed between her legs and fucked the woman that he planned to spend the rest of his life with like she owed him five month's rent.

"Oh my god baby! Remember that it's your pussy! You're going to kill me!" Angela squealed as he pummeled her mercilessly, swatting away her hand as she tried to restrain him.

Angela bit into a pillow hard as he flooded her insides with his juices, triggering her own orgasm. She ripped the pillow and its case with her teeth like a wild animal as she convulsed and shook like a woman possessed.

She wondered if she would ever be able to get used to the insane intensity she felt whenever she had sex with Jerome. She transformed into a carnal beast whenever he was inside her. It was scary and liberating at the same time. She sighed contentedly as she threw the damaged pillow to the floor and snuggled up against him. All she had wanted was a quickie but instead Jerome had fucked her into next month. She felt deliciously drained. She was so tired. He hugged her and she closed her eyes.

She didn't open them again for the rest of the night.

Dr. Muirhead slipped on his spectacles and glanced at the time before answering the phone. Ten p.m. He was in bed reading a psychology journal. He looked at the caller ID. It was a private number. He answered the call.

"Hello, Dr. Muirhead here."

"Hi, Doctor. It's Sara Charlton."

"Hello Sara," he responded, closing the journal and placing it on the bedside table.

"I know it's late but you said to call you anytime I needed to talk outside of our sessions..."

"No, no, no need to apologize. I'm happy that you called," he reassured her. He had been treating Sara for two weeks now. And after six two-hour long sessions, he was finally getting somewhere. The last two sessions had been particularly progressive. She had finally opened up and told him everything. From her promiscuity and sleeping with her sister's boyfriends, to the strained relationship with her family, to the brutal rape that she had endured.

Truth was indeed stranger than fiction. Her story was a very interesting one. Sara was a very troubled young lady and his heart went out to her beyond a professional level. Underneath all the pain and anger was a beautiful young woman who had a lot to offer the world. And the right man. He was surprised to find himself so attracted to her. In eight years of practice he had never considered going there with a patient before.

Maybe the recent separation from his wife, Renita, who despite having been caught in a compromising situation with a senior police detective, was giving him a hard time by contesting the divorce, had left him more vulnerable than he had realized. Sara was sixteen years his junior, and her mental state was akin to that of road-kill. He would have to be careful not to take advantage of her.

He was shocked when he got off the phone and looked at the time. It was a few minutes past midnight. They had been on the phone for over two hours. He sighed as he turned off the bedside lamp and stared at the ceiling in the dark. Falling for Sara Charlton like a smitten schoolboy was a very bad idea on many levels. He would have to keep his emotions in check.

He thought about her until he fell asleep.

CHAPTER 4

Jerome surveyed the crowd as he sipped his Hennessy and red bull, and smoked some weed. In a show of respect to Lenky, a multitude of people had turned out for Mikey's wake. A long line of vehicles were parked along the stretch of road in the upscale neighbourhood. There were people there from all walks of life: gangsters, cops, disc jockeys, businessmen, a doctor, a lawyer, a politician or two. Lenky's criminal tentacles spread far and wide, and he had connections in every facet of society. Mikey wasn't well liked by any means, and the majority of the people present didn't give two fucks that he was dead.

He was sitting beside Lenky, who was listening to members of their inner circle swap stories about Mikey. Lenky's eyes, no doubt swollen and red from crying, were hidden behind Cavalli shades. He was dressed in full black, as he had been all week.

There was some tension in the air between some of the women present. Jada and one of her home girls had been scowling at Laura every time they saw her while Laura looked coldly at Michelle whenever they made eye contact. Angela had asked him if he wanted her to come to the wake but he told her no. There were too many women here that he had fucked or was currently seeing. Having Angela here would be tempting fate. He wouldn't bring her to the funeral either. Thinking about her made him miss her. He whipped out his phone and sent her a text.

Laura sighed as she peed, wiped and flushed. The week had flown by quickly and for that she was grateful. She just wished that tonight would go by as speedily. She couldn't wait for Mikey to be buried so that things could get back to normal. She was tired of having to run around dealing with everything. Lenky would stop moping and start handling his business and she could focus on what's important, like how she was going to get rid of the baby without arousing Lenky's suspicion. She was already doing a good job of pretending that she wanted it, now she just had to lose it and make it seem like she had a miscarriage.

She washed and dried her hands, and looked at herself in the full length mirror. She rubbed her stomach and sighed. She wasn't ready to be a mother but it would have been so nice to have Jerome's baby. She was positive that it was his. But Lenky would kill them both. She had to get rid of it. And Jerome was going to have to help her to do it.

She took a last look at her face, and reassured that her make up didn't need retouching, made her way back downstairs. She heard voices in the kitchen and went to look who was in there.

She stopped at the doorway and a look of disgust clouded her pretty face.

It was Jada, Lenky's ghetto ass baby mother, and one of her friends.

Elizabeth Rhoden was on her knees on the plush white carpet in the den. She was nude except for her black stilettos and thigh high black stockings. A dildo was buried deep inside her depths, the purple end of it extending from her pussy. Her husband was relaxing on the couch, a glass of Moet in one hand, his dick in the other, watching and stroking as she went around the semi-circle of four men, spending a few minutes sucking each of their dicks.

She tried not to gag as she fellated Christoph Ballack, a German manufacturer who was visiting Jamaica to close a business deal with her husband. He was well hung and he stank. A very stifling combination. One of the men moved behind her and after a few seconds, she could feel his hot semen on her back.

After three weeks of constant humiliation and degradation at the hands of her husband, she was now numb and did his disgusting bidding with a detached air, as though she was watching someone else in action. She had arrived at a decision two days ago when he had put her through the most degrading act that she had ever engaged in. Something had died in her that night and she knew that to save herself she had to do something. And soon. She could not continue like this. But she could not divorce him as because of the ironclad prenuptial agreement that she had signed, she would get nothing of consequence.

There was only one thing left to do.

She closed her eyes as the German ejaculated.

"What the fuck are you doing in my house?" Laura asked, with her hands on her hips. "There's no reason for you to be inside here. Food and liquor is outside, and the bathrooms by the pool house are open for use. Get the fuck out!"

Jada scowled at her.

"Goweh dutty gal, this is my man's house, so fuck you and the high horse yuh ride in on," Jada sneered, looking at Laura with pure hatred.

"You fucking low class bitch," Laura growled as she moved threateningly towards Jada. "I'm going to slap the shit outta your skinny, ugly ass."

"Come try dutty gal!" Jada retorted. She put down her bottle of beer on the kitchen counter and advanced towards Laura.

Laura grabbed a skillet from off of the hook on the wall in stride. Jada stopped in her tracks and leaned back to avoid the hit but it was too late. Laura smacked Jada flush in the forehead, knocking her to the ground.

Blacka, who had come inside to fetch another bottle of Hennessy for Lenky, was shocked to see Laura standing over Jada with her arm raised, ready to bash Jada's face in with the skillet. Jada's friend was just standing there, watching with her mouth open.

He moved over to Laura and held her hand.

"Yuh shouldn't be upsetting yourself," he gently chided, taking the skillet away from her. "Yuh have to think about the baby."

Laura sighed and tried to calm down. She couldn't believe that Jada had the nerve to come inside her home and disrespect her. She was sorry that she didn't get the chance to hit her again but the first blow had connected nicely. There was already a large lump on Jada's forehead.

Laura nodded, smirked at Jada, who was still on the floor, her teary eyes blazing with unadulterated hate, and went outside via the living room exit.

Blacka helped up Jada.

"Yuh mad? How yuh must pick fight with the boss pregnant wife?" he asked. "If Lenky ever hear about this, mi sorry for yuh."

Jada sucked her teeth and shook her hand free from his grasp. Her forehead throbbed painfully. She grimaced as she gently touched the lump. Blacka was right though. Lenky would place the blame for the altercation squarely at her feet and would give her a sound beating.

Jada sighed in frustration and left the kitchen. She didn't even look at Karen, her friend. The bitch hadn't even helped her. She decided to go home. She made her way through the throng of people and went out to where her car was parked on the street.

She didn't look back to see if Karen was following.

CHAPTER 5

"Jah know 'Rome...yuh is a true friend," Lenky was saying to Jerome. "Yuh really help me to get through this rough time. Mi really appreciate it."

Their glasses of Hennessy and red bull clinked in a toast to their friendship.

"That's what friends are for," Jerome responded. "Have to be there for each other in times of need."

"Yuh have a clean heart Jerome, don't ever change and make success get to your head," Lenky continued.

Jerome nodded, feeling a small pang of guilt when he glanced at Laura, who was sitting at the other end of the pool talking to a girl that he didn't recognize. Lenky considered him to be his best friend yet he was fucking the man's wife. Possibly had gotten her pregnant. That was some foul shit. But what to do? Everything had happened so fast and when he met her he didn't know that she was Lenky's wife. *But when you found out you didn't stop now did you?* He looked away and sipped his drink. His mobile vibrated in the pocket of his jeans, temporarily silencing the little voice in his head. He checked the caller ID. It was a private number.

"Hello."

"Hi, is this Jerome?" The voice was sultry, melodic. Slightly familiar.

"Yeah...who is this?"

"Cheetah."

Oh shit. The singer. He didn't bother to ask her how she got his number.

"Hi sexy...what's up?"

"You. Are you busy? I just finished up at the studio and I have the rest of the night free until I leave for Philadelphia tomorrow morning at nine."

Jerome smiled. The alcohol and marijuana had him feeling very horny. He had planned to spend the night with Angela but this was too good an opportunity to pass up.

"Sure, you can see me," he responded. "I'm at a wake up by Cherry Gardens at my friend's house."

Cheetah was turned on by his nonchalant tone. A man who was used to premium pussy being offered to him. A welcome change from easily impressed men who were always drooling over her. She asked him for the address and if it was okay for her to bring her stuff and spend the entire night with him. Jerome told her no problem and that he would take her to the airport in the morning. She hung up after telling him that she would be there in another hour and a half.

Jerome looked at the time. It was 10:45 p.m.

He called Angela to let her know that he would be spending the night at Lenky's.

Karen, Jada's friend, went out to the street to look for Jada when she didn't see her return after several minutes had passed. Jada's red Honda Civic was nowhere in sight. Karen was sure that it had been parked behind the white Mini Cooper. Damn. She couldn't believe that Jada had left without telling her. How was she going to get home? She didn't know anyone else here and didn't have enough money to catch a cab to get home.

She whipped out her mobile and dialed Jada's number. She answered on the fourth ring.

"What?"

"Why you go away and leave me like that?" Karen asked.

"You lucky...why you just stand up there and watch the gal lick me inna mi head wid de frying pan? Find your own rass way home!" Jada growled, and ended the call.

Karen couldn't believe that Jada was mad at her for not intervening. Everything had happened so fast. What could she possibly have done? Sucking her teeth at Jada's unfairness, she made her way back inside. She went by the bar and asked for a rum and coke. She then wandered through the crowd aimlessly, pondering her next move.

She saw Laura on a lounge chair by the pool in animated conversation with a slender, attractive girl. She made a beeline to the other side of the pool, not wanting Laura to see her and possibly embarrass her by saying something or worse.

She just wanted to go home. She looked over where Lenky was sitting, surrounded by his friends and henchmen. The football star was over there, as was the guy that had broken up the scuffle between Jada and Laura in the kitchen. He was staring at her. He was one of the darkest persons that she had ever seen. Dressed in full black, he was only visible from where he was sitting because of the light and his big bright eyes. She held his gaze. He said something to the guy next to him, and ambled over to her, his drink and marijuana joint in hand.

"Yuh is Jada friend." More of a statement than a question.

"Yeah," Karen responded. "I'm Karen."

"Ah me name Blacka," he said, as though she was supposed to have heard of him.

He took her free hand and rubbed it. She tried not to grimace. His hand was as coarse as sandpaper. "So how come yuh just walking around like a lost sheep...where's Jada?"

"She went home," Karen responded, wishing that he'd stop rubbing her hand. But she said nothing, and did not pull her hand away. It wouldn't do to offend him.

Blacka's large intense eyes were roaming all over her body. The predatory way in which he was looking at her made her feel like her tight denim jeans and baby T had been discarded and she was standing there in all her naked glory.

"How yuh getting home? Yuh drive?" he asked, taking a sip of his drink.

"I don't know...no, I need a ride," she responded.

Blacka smiled. His teeth were as black as the rest of him.

"Come chill with me until yuh ready to go home. I'll drop yuh there." He turned and walked away, expecting her to follow him. After a moment's hesitation she did, albeit reluctantly. She knew exactly where this was heading. And she felt powerless to stop it.

Karen followed Blacka inside the house and he led her around to one of the bedrooms on the ground floor that he sometimes slept in when he had to stay over. He kept the lights off and only a wee bit of moonlight filtering in through the open window prevented the room from being pitch black. Karen wanted to tell him that she wasn't up for this but when he removed a large chrome handgun from his waist and placed it on the bedside table, any objection to what was about to happen died in her throat.

His drink and the marijuana joint, which apparently had gone out as it wasn't burning, joined the gun on the bedside table. Silent, he then quickly removed his clothing and looked at her expectantly. Karen, near tears, sat on the bed and struggled to take off her hard to remove jeans. This wasn't exactly rape, and she had not said no, but they both knew that the situation would turn ugly in a heartbeat if she refused to have sex with him.

When she was finally naked, he pulled her towards him and holding on to both her shoulders, pushed her downwards. Karen's tears vacated her eyes and trickled down her cheeks as took him inside her mouth, praying that she wouldn't throw up and that he would see that she was no good at giving head and make her get up.

His dick grew in her mouth and he groaned, holding the back of her head in place as he stroked her mouth, pushing it in all the way to the back of her throat. When he finally allowed her some breathing space, she gasped loudly, wiped the excess saliva from her mouth with the back of her hand, and tried to catch her breath. After a few minutes of more of the same, he finally pulled her up. He made her bend over the side of the bed and when she asked him to put on a condom; he sucked his teeth and squeezing her throat with one hand, entered her dryness with a firm thrust.

He was rough and he couldn't fuck. Karen prayed that he would quickly have an orgasm. He was like a jack rabbit on steroids, no technique, except to go as fast as he possibly could. She continued to pray that he would climax quickly. If only Jada had not unfairly left her behind, especially seeing as she had picked her up from her home after asking her to accompany her. And now this was happening to her. She would never forgive Jada for this.

The bedroom door opened and Ping Pong slipped inside the room. Blacka had told him that if he wanted some of the action he should come to the room a few minutes after he saw him go into the house with the girl.

He removed his clothing and waited for Blacka to finish. He chuckled to himself as he watched. Blacka was so dark that it was almost as though no one was behind the woman.

She looked like she was being fucked by a ghost.

CHAPTER 6

"I'm here," Cheetah announced, when Jerome answered the phone. He excused himself from his conversation with Lenky and went around to the front to meet her. She exited the grey double cab Toyota Tundra that was idling just inside the driveway and a guy came out to help her with the two suitcases.

She hugged Jerome when he came over.

"Mmmm...so nice seeing you again..." she whispered in his ear.

Jerome smiled. She felt and smelled really good. He loved the scent that she was wearing. He would have to find out the name of it and get one for Angela.

"Same here sexy..." he responded, brushing her right cheek with his lips.

She reluctantly removed herself from his arms and took up the small suitcase, while Jerome hoisted the bigger one.

"I'll see you tomorrow Rocky," she said over her shoulder to her manager. He nodded and drove off, shaking his head in disappointment. Some guys had all the luck. He had been her manager for eight months and though she wasn't in a serious relationship and they spent a lot of time together, he hadn't even come close to sniffing her panties much less getting in them.

Yet she met this guy four days ago, and this was only the second time that she was seeing him, and she was more than ready to offer herself to him on a platter. She had been in the truck squirming like a bitch in heat. She was a rising star and was here acting like a groupie.

Rocky shook his head in disgust.

Jerome led her to the bedroom he slept in whenever he stayed over at Lenky's. No one else had been allowed to use it since Jerome and Lenky became best friends. He deposited her Louis Vuitton suitcase on the carpeted floor. Cheetah was looking at him when he straightened up and turned around. Her pretty face was clouded with desire. Sex oozed from her pores.

"Damn you're hot. Even hotter than I remembered. My pussy is playing hop scotch right now Jerome. It wants you inside it."

Jerome reached down and rubbed her crotch through her striped leggings. He groaned. It was soaked. And plump. Just the way he liked it.

Cheetah's eyes were tiny slits. Her breathing became ragged. Jerome ended his caress with a gentle squeeze.

"Soon...let's go get a drink...and I want you to meet my friend."

Cheetah followed him outside, marveling at his coolness. Any other guy would've been all over her immediately. He was such a turn on. Her pussy was so wet she was convinced that she would be dehydrated before they got back to the bedroom.

All eyes were on them as they maneuvered through the crowd and made their way over to Lenky. Michelle, who was standing with a group of people in the entertainment industry, watched in surprise as Cheetah walked by with Jerome. *Damn...she sure didn't waste any time,* she mused in annoyance. But what could she do? Jerome didn't belong to her. She had to be content with just getting a piece of him like everybody else. It wasn't his fault that she was in love with him. He had promised her nothing. She just had to suck it up and deal with it.

Laura's mood soured when she saw Jerome with the pretty girl that she did not recognize. Was that his girl-friend? Why did he bring her here? Did he not care about her feelings? The questions came hard and fast, and by the time Jerome had introduced the girl to Lenky, her night was ruined. She was certifiably pissed. And there was nothing that she could do about it.

"Isn't that the singer with the number one song on the local charts?" Khianna asked her. "Cheetah I think her name is."

Laura didn't respond. She merely scowled as she watched Jerome pour a glass of champagne and hand it to the girl. She had to admit, the girl was very pretty and sexy. Almost like a more petite version of her. She felt threatened. She had to find out if that was his woman and why he had brought her here.

Khianna noticed the change in Laura's mood and it was obvious that it had something to do with the girl and the football star. She wondered what that was about but didn't dare ask. Laura wasn't the kind of person that you asked personal questions and the last thing she wanted was to get on her shit list. She lit a cigarette and changed the subject.

"Take me home now please," Karen sobbed. After an hour of sex, Blacka had her twice and Ping Pong once, she had taken a shower and gotten dressed. She was embarrassed, sore and distraught. The two men had had their way with her against her will. Though she had not said no, she knew it would have happened regardless, but accompanied with violence if she had protested. These men were killers. And she was in their lair. No was not an option, at least in their eyes. There had been no choice but to quietly comply. At least she hadn't been battered and bruised, or worse, killed.

They looked at her, smirking, presumably amused by her tears.

"What yuh crying for?" Blacka queried, sticking his gun inside the waist of his jeans. "Yuh never enjoy it?"

Ping Pong chuckled as he took out a bag from his pocket and doled out some marijuana to Blacka along with a strip of rolling paper.

Karen tried to suppress the bile in her throat. She felt sick. She didn't respond. She hugged herself tightly and waited for them to do as she asked.

"Alright," Blacka conceded, "mi did promise to carry yuh home...plus the pussy kinda good so mi will keep mi promise."

Ping Pong found this hilarious and laughed heartily.

Karen trooped behind them as they exited the house. She would never speak to Jada again. Because of her unfairness, she had left her stranded miles away from home, resulting in these animals employed by her baby father taking advantage of her. What kind of friend would do such a thing?

The experience had left a nasty stain on her soul.

She wondered if she would ever be able to remove it.

After Cheetah had two glasses of champagne and Jerome had three more drinks of Hennessy and red bull, and another marijuana joint, they excused themselves and made their way inside. Jerome glimpsed

Laura in his periphery but did not look over there. He knew that she was pissed and was battling to control herself from reacting. Laura was something else. He was sure that she would fight Cheetah right this minute if she could. The irony of her getting upset over him having sex with another woman in her husband's house was not lost on him. He knew that he was going to get an earful from her as soon as she got the chance to talk to him in private.

He brushed thoughts of Laura aside when they entered the room. It was time to focus on the matter at hand. The alcohol and weed were raging in his system. He was rearing to go. So was Cheetah. By the time he switched on the bedside lamp and removed his shirt and loafers, Cheetah was already naked. She helped him out of his jeans and boxers.

"Oh. My. God." Cheetah whispered in awe when his dick uncoiled from his boxers like an angry cobra. "Are you fucking serious? A dick cannot be this big...look at the veins...damn..."

"Scared?" Jerome teased as he gripped a fistful of her silky weave and pulled her to him, their faces an inch apart.

"The only thing I'm scared of is poverty," she replied, her green contacts blazing in the soft light as she looked deep inside his soul. "I've never fucked a man this fast before and I've never had a dick this big but I like to experience new things...its good for my art."

Jerome chuckled. He was going to give her some inspiration all right. He was going to ensure that the next song she wrote would be about him. Their lips met and Cheetah whimpered in his mouth as he kissed her deeply, their tongues entwined like Siamese twins. Jerome caressed her back and ass as he explored her mouth hungrily. Cheetah swooned against him, her knees weak from passion, when he slipped a solitary finger inside her wetness from behind. Cheetah groaned and clutched him tightly as he slipped another finger in.

Cheetah's delicate chest heaved as she tried to catch her breath when Jerome finally broke the kiss. He removed his fingers and placed them on her lips. She took them in her mouth.

"Music...put some music on Jerome...I'm really loud when I'm enjoying sex and something tells me I'm going to be louder than I've ever been tonight," she breathed, removing his fingers and going over to the bed, collapsing on it. He was just getting warmed up and already he had her feeling dizzy with desire.

Jerome went over to the small but expensive CD player on the bedside table and turned it on. He pressed play, adjusted the volume and the thumping bass line of a dancehall rhythm filled the room.

Cheetah pivoted on the bed and Jerome moved over to her. She grasped his shaft with both hands, drooled on it, and then stroked it lovingly until it was as hard as marble. Jerome groaned as she ran her tongue along its length, licking him slowly, from his scrotum to the bulbous head; and back again.

She then took him halfway into her mouth, moaning loudly as sucked him languidly, wrapping her pierced tongue around his dick like a snake around its prey. Jerome gripped her hair tightly, painfully. She loved it. Her moans got louder. She twisted her body and reached down between her legs with her free hand. Her head bobbed furiously as if competing with the hand rubbing her engorged clit.

"Ahhhhh...mmmmm...ohhhh..." she moaned as she climaxed, removing his dick from her mouth and stroking it languidly.

"I'm ready Jerome...come and fuck me...hard...I want you to puncture my lungs with that monster..." she told him, licking her luscious lips as she looked at him with tortured want. "Fuck me as hard as you want...pain turns me on..."

Jerome muttered an unintelligible response and quickly retrieved a condom from the bedside table drawer.

He rolled it on and positioned Cheetah at the edge of the bed. She propped herself up on her elbows and watched with baited breath as Jerome placed his dick at the entrance of her anxiously awaiting pussy. He held it there and looked at her.

"Give it to me Jerome," she growled. Her voice was unrecognizable.

Jerome entered her with a hard thrust, burying it to the hilt.

The squeal that escaped Cheetah's lip gloss coated lips would put a pig to shame.

Jerome stroked Cheetah deep and hard, bending over, holding her firmly in place as he introduced her to some new pleasure points located deep inside her.

"Oh God! Fuck me! Fuck me Jerome! Yes! Yes!" she shouted as she pounded his muscular back with her fists. "It hurts so fucking good! Oh God! Ripping me apart! Don't stop!"

Jerome didn't. He clicked into high gear and the bed shook mightily from the force of his exertions.

"Oh Lord have mercy...I'm coming...my pussy feels like its going explode Jerome...I'm coming! I'm coming! Arggghhhhhhh!"

Cheetah wrapped her long legs around his back tightly, holding him in a tight embrace and screamed as the most intense orgasm she had ever had in her twenty-three years shook her so hard that her teeth rattled.

When her orgasm finally subsided, Jerome pulled out of her and dragged her from off of the bed.

"Stand up," he commanded.

She did, albeit unsteadily, and he got behind her in a wide-legged stance. Bending her over slightly, he entered her and pulled her hands behind her, holding on to her wrists to prevent her from toppling over.

"Ugh! Ugh! Ugh!" Cheetah grunted with each vicious plunge. "I feel it in my throat!"

She started moving forward with each stroke, and he moved with her, drilling her relentlessly. They got to the door and he released her hands so that she could brace against the door for balance, and slapped her ass cheeks mercilessly with each thrust.

Cheetah's eyes rolled to the back of her head. He was fucking her so hard she was sure that her contacts had fallen out. The pain was damn near excruciating. The pleasure was mind-boggling. The result was orgasmic. She hit a high note like she was on stage performing as she climaxed hard, her center feeling like it had exploded into a thousand tiny pieces. Pain enhanced her pleasure. And Jerome had the perfect mix. One man should not be able to fuck this good. To be so perfectly able to deliver exactly what was needed. It was too much power for one man to have. She needed to stop screaming now, she had a show in Philadelphia tomorrow night and she couldn't afford to lose her voice. Try telling that to her orgasm.

It was behaving as though it didn't plan to end.

Laura, standing outside the door, summoned all of her will power not to go inside the room. She had deliberately walked through that section of the house on her way upstairs. Why she was torturing herself like this she had no idea. Jerome was in her house fucking the stuffing out of that tramp and there was nothing that she could do about it. She gritted her teeth and stormed upstairs, the girl's orgasmic screams mockingly ringing in her ears.

CHAPTER 7

"**N**eed more juice?" Angela asked, as she got up to go to the refrigerator to get some for herself. Jerome downed the contents of his glass and handed it her. He smacked her on the ass as she walked by, almost causing her to drop the glasses.

"Baby!" she chided, though she loved it.

After dropping Cheetah off at the airport, Jerome went home to shower, change, drink a protein shake and then head over to Angela's so that he could spend a couple of hours with her before Mikey's funeral.

She returned to the table with the two glasses of cranberry juice.

"So I'm having dinner with my family this evening," she said, sitting down across from him.

"Cool...tell everyone hello for me. How is Sara doing?"

Angela sipped her juice before responding.

"Much better," she replied. "The therapy seems to be working."

"That's great." Jerome was thoughtful as he took a bite of his roast beef sandwich. He still harboured a slight fear of Angela finding out that he had slept with Sara. He knew that their mother wouldn't breathe a word but Sara was unpredictable. The rape had healed the rift in the family but Jerome knew that not all fences remain mended. But it was useless to worry about it. He could only remain positive and hope for the best.

He smiled seductively at Angela. She blushed.

"I love you baby," he told her. She looked so radiant and beautiful. Happiness was truly the best cosmetic for beauty.

"Awww I love you more honey," she gushed.

Jerome checked his watch to see if he had enough time for a quickie. Though Cheetah had given him an extensive work out last night, Angela was wearing a pair of really cute boy shorts that perfectly displayed her curvy yet petite figure. He wanted her.

"Come here," he said hoarsely.

She happily did so.

The funeral was a somber affair but there was very little crying. Even Lenky, seated between Laura and Jerome, and oblivious to the tension between them, surprisingly, did not cry. Perhaps he was all cried out. The church was hot but the service was mercifully short. The Minister that Lenky had paid and rented the church from for the service had been asked to keep it brief but he didn't need to be told. He couldn't wait to get rid of these gangsters out of his church. As to the one that was being buried, he was a known killer, and a despicable human being. Ordinarily he would have declined, but these were tough times, and he needed four new tires for his car. Every dollar counted.

Jerome, who was asked by Lenky to be one of the pall bearers, assumed his position along with Lenky and the other four men at the coffin, and they led the procession out into the church yard. It was a sunny Sunday afternoon, and the sun beamed down brilliantly on the crowd, most of whom were dressed in black. Once the coffin was inside the hearse, Jerome, Laura and Lenky climbed into Lenky's Lincoln Navigator. Blacka drove with Laura in the front, while Lenky and Jerome rode in the back. The funeral procession, escorted by four policemen who regularly worked for Lenky, got to the cemetery in half an hour.

The pall bearers took the coffin to the grave site under the watchful eye of the undertaker and the coffin was placed on the straps above the grave. Everyone gathered around and the Pastor led them in song as the coffin was lowered into the earth.

Jerome felt a sudden pang of sadness as he thought about his mother and grandmother. It had been seven years since the arson that claimed their lives yet the pain was still as fresh as if it had happened yesterday. Jerome sighed. Life was fleeting. One minute you were here and the next you were gone, forever. Live each day as if it was your last. Such a cliché, but like most clichés, there was an element of truth in it.

You never knew when you were going to go.

Ashes to ashes, dust to dust.

He watched as Lenky stooped down, took up a handful of dirt, and threw it on the coffin.

Cheetah sucked on a Strepsil as she thumbed through a fashion magazine. She was in first class on her flight to Philadelphia. She was slightly hoarse from her incredible night with Jerome and needed to get her voice on track for her show tonight. She wished that she was sucking on Jerome's dick. His sweet, gigantic lollipop that he had used to abuse her pussy. She was sore and aching. She loved the feeling. Pain was her pleasure. It had always been like that for as long as she could remember. As a child she used to be rude just so that her mom would slap her. It felt good. She had three tattoos in very sensitive areas and had climaxed each time from the pain.

But nothing compared to sexual pain. And when it was the right kind of pain, the resulting orgasms were indescribable. And no one had ever given her the kind of orgasms that Jerome did. She was wet just thinking about it. Her sexual juices weren't the only juices flowing though. She was going to head to the studio as soon as she arrived in Philadelphia. Jerome had inspired a song. The words and the melody were all in her head.

She was going to call it *Pleasurable Pain.*

CHAPTER 8

The man entered the house through the helper's quarters at the rear, next to the back patio. It was her weekend off and the one who covered for her at such times lived in Kingston and was not required to stay on the premises. He proceeded slowly but methodically, the flashlight and his memory of the layout of the house guiding him.

He had been given a quick tour on Friday evening; right after the helper had left work at five. He gripped the flashlight and his weapon, a combat knife, tightly as he navigated the long passage and entered the living room. The beam from his flashlight revealed a 72 inch plasma TV, plush wall to wall carpeting, chandeliers, exquisite antique furniture, sculptures and weird looking art – in his estimation anyway – on the walls. The room reeked of wealth. Wealth that he craved. Wealth that he was about to obtain. If she thought that he was going to stick to the agreed sum, she had another thing coming.

He might just be a handyman, and not a very good one at that, but he wasn't stupid. She was about to have access to millions of dollars, surely getting that access was worth much more than two hundred and fifty thousand. Much more. He climbed the stairs, adrenaline pumping faster through his veins with each step. He felt nervous when he got to the top of the stairs. He closed his eyes and thought of how the money would change his life. That steadied his nerves somewhat and he continued on, freezing in shock as his elbow inadvertently hit a vase, sending it crashing to the floor.

"What the hell was that?" Ralph Rhoden asked, jumping out of his sleep. He roused his wife, shaking her roughly. She opened her eyes slowly and frowned, rubbing them, as if she had been in a deep sleep.

Ralph switched on the bedside lamp.

"Did you hear that sound?" He threw the covers aside and hopped out of the bed. "I think there's someone in the house."

"Don't be ridiculous Ralph...the alarm would've went off if someone had tried to break in," Elizabeth responded, getting up and slipping on her robe. She was naked underneath. She always slept in the nude.

Ralph ignored her and retrieved his licensed .38 revolver from the bedside table drawer and made his way to the door.

Elizabeth's heart pounded between her fake breasts. This was supposed to be so easy, yet the idiot had managed to make a mess of it by hitting over something in the passageway. Most likely the Tibetan vase that was at the top of the staircase. Now that Ralph was alert and armed, anything could happen.

"Stay here!" her husband hissed, as he slowly opened the bedroom door.

She rushed to him and held on to him as he opened the door.

"No Ralph, I'm scared!" she said loudly, hoping to alert Nyron, the gardener.

Her husband turned his head and tried to shove her away.

"Be quiet woman," he spat, annoyed at her stupidity. If someone was out there they would be aware that the noise had been heard.

He turned around just in time to see the glint of the blade as it plunged into his chest. The pain was excruciating. His attacker held on to the knife, twisting it cruelly. Ralph Rhoden screamed at the top of his lungs. He placed both hands on his attacker's, then realizing that he still held the gun, squeezed the trigger.

Nyron grunted and backed away slowly, holding his stomach. Ralph fired again and again. Nyron staggered back, his face a mask of disbelief and pain, as he toppled over the railing and fell twenty-five feet below, smashing into a small glass table that housed several photos of the Rhoden's posing with famous people.

Elizabeth, feeling sick from all the blood but excited at the way that things had turned out, slowly went over to the phone and called the police. She didn't have to. She could hear sirens approaching by the time she hung up the phone. This was an exclusive neighbourhood and most likely one of the neighbours had called the police the second they had heard the sound of gunfire.

Ralph was now on the floor, choking on his own blood. Elizabeth sat on the floor and cradled his head in her lap, trying not to vomit at the gruesome sight. The sirens were now at her gate. She got up and opened the gate, using the keypad on the bedroom wall, then went downstairs to meet them.

She glanced at Nyron, dead on the floor with broken glass all around him, his neck at an awkward angle. She hoped that by the time the police got upstairs her husband would be dead too. She was giddy with excitement. She had actually pulled it off and because of Nyron's ineptness, things had turned out better than she could have ever imagined. Nyron was dead too. Not only would she not have to pay him any money, she did not have to worry about him ever breathing a word of their plan to anyone. He had taken their deadly secret into the afterlife.

She took a deep breath and summoned tears as she opened the door for the police.

It was time to put on the performance of her life.

CHAPTER 9

The news of Ralph Rhoden's murder swept the city of Kingston, and indeed the entire Jamaica on Monday morning, sending shock-waves through the business community. He was a very prominent businessman and was highly respected in the private sector.

Jerome heard about it on his way home after his morning jog at Emancipation Park. He stopped at a gas station to purchase a bottle of water, and after exchanging pleasantries with the female clerk who had recognized him and was an avid football fan; he paid for the water and immediately took a long swig, downing half of it.

He was about to leave when the news of Ralph Rhoden's murder came on over the radio. According to the reporter, a senior cop, who spoke on condition of anonymity, said that Mr. Rhoden was stabbed and murdered in his home by a gardener in his employ at 2 a.m. this morning. The gardener had broken into the house and attacked Mr. Rhoden who had managed to discharge his firearm and shoot the assailant before succumbing to his injuries. His wife, Elizabeth, was there but was not harmed, though obviously traumatized and suffering from severe shock. The reporter then went on to state that the police were still carrying out investigations and an official statement would be provided to the public at midday.

Jerome exited the store in a slight daze. He remembered when he had met Ralph Rhoden at the Jamaica Football Association headquarters several weeks ago. He had been convinced that the man knew that he was sleeping with his wife. Jerome thought of Elizabeth as he neared his apartment. She was a now a widow. A wealthy, traumatized widow. He could only imagine how devastated she was after surviving such a horrible life-changing experience.

Though she had turned him off with her possessive attitude and he had lost interest, he felt compelled to contact her and give her his condolences. It was probably too soon to give her a call but he would definitely do so tomorrow.

"Oh my God!" Angela exclaimed in horror. She was driving to the office and had just heard the news on the radio. She shook her head in disgust as she listened to the details. Wow. She couldn't imagine going through something like that, witnessing her husband get murdered in their home. Her heart went out to Elizabeth Rhoden. Though there was no love lost between them, as the woman had been very rude to her, she felt really sorry for her loss. Ralph Rhoden had been a client of hers for close to a year, and after she had warned him to stop his advances or she would stop treating him, he had behaved himself and she had found him to be a very pleasant man. Her cell phone rang. She pressed the answer button on her Bluetooth. It was Jerome. He was calling to see if she had heard the ghastly news. They chatted until she got to the office.

Lenky woke up at 9 a.m. He glanced at his wife. She was fast asleep, a strange expression on her face. He loved her so much. She had been wonderful and attentive since Mikey's untimely passing. And she had his seed in her stomach. He had lost his brother but would soon gain a daughter. He rose and swung his legs to the carpeted floor. He looked down, staring for a long time as though the answers to life's mysteries were in the plush white carpet. Mikey was gone. Laid to rest in fine style. It was now time to pull himself together and get things back on track. There were decisions to be made, people to see and money to make. Life goes on. He got up and went into the bathroom to take a shower.

Elizabeth took a sip of her bottled water and looked at the senior detective steadily.

"Am I a suspect, Detective Spence?" she asked, getting fed up of having to answer the same questions over and over again. She had already given a detailed statement to the first set of cops to arrive at the crime scene. They had been nice enough to allow her to stay home and do it instead of going down to the police station. The family attorney had been present to offer moral support. Her physician had come by and given her some medication to help her sleep and upon waking up, this asshole cop had come by unannounced, asking to speak with her briefly.

"Of course not, Mrs. Rhoden," he replied, after a pregnant pause. *And its Detecetive Corporal Spence to you, you arrogant bitch.* He had his doubts, but there wasn't anything that he could about it. How did the gardener get inside the house? There was no sign of forced entry and the house had an impressive security system that somehow, had not raised an alarm. His instincts told him that this was not the open and shut case that his superiors thought and were ready to declare that it was. But he had to tread carefully. The Rhoden name was highly connect-ed and respected. No one would want to hear that he suspected that the wife had played a part in her husband's murder. He would be putting his career in jeopardy, and he didn't have any proof. He had questioned the helper who was on duty the evening of the murder but was satisfied that the poor girl was not in cahoots with the gardener.

"If that is all, I'm afraid I need to go and rest," Elizabeth told him, rising.

The meeting was over.

Spence rose and thanked her for her time. She told him that the helper would see him out and exit-ed the room. He breathed in the faint whiff of per-fume that she had left behind. She was a very attractive woman. And a very wealthy one. The helper, a rather tall dour faced woman, escorted him to the door.

He slipped on his shades as he stepped out into the brilliant mid morning sunshine and made his way to his car. He looked up at the large house when he got inside the car. Mrs. Rhoden was standing by a window upstairs, watching him. He couldn't read her expression. He gave her a little wave as he drove off. She didn't wave back.

His instincts were never wrong. He wasn't buying the theory that the gardener had sneaked into the house just before the helper left and then hid until 2 a.m. before making his move. That just didn't make any sense. He lit a cigarette as he took a left turn when he got to the bottom of the hill. It was useless thinking about it. The top brass had internally ruled the case as a homicide. Open and shut. They would not tolerate anyone second guessing and showing them up. Especially in a high profile murder such as this. When he thought about his superiors one thing always came to mind. *In an organization, every employee rises to his level of incompetence.* No wonder the poor country was going to shit.

God bless Jamaica.

CHAPTER 10

"Oh God! Damn I missed you! Ughhhh! Fuck!" Tara groaned loudly as she bounced up and down Jerome's light pole. Her frayed Juicy Couture denim skirt was bunched around her waist, and her striped pink and white Victoria Secret panties were pulled to the side of her quivering mound. Her full breasts jiggled underneath her fitted graphic T-shirt as she soared to cloud nine. Jerome was laying on his back on the living room floor. Tara had been too horny to make it any further when she got inside the house. She had just gotten back from Miami where she had gone to attend a cousin's wedding. She was the maid of honour and had been there for a week. Jerome was all she had thought about. And now he was inside her, filling her up and taking her to places that only he could.

She shuddered uncontrollably as she climaxed, screaming his name over and over again. Jerome didn't wait for her orgasm to subside before changing positions. His dick still deeply embedded inside her, he flipped her onto her side and raised her right leg, holding it high in the air for more leverage. Tara could see their reflection through the glass on the entertainment centre. The sight of her pussy obscenely exposed, being drilled into submission by Jerome's massive shaft triggered another orgasm. It was a sunny Monday morning, and all the sunshine seemed to be emanating from between her legs.

She howled with pleasure from the intensity of her back to back orgasms. Jerome then placed her on her knees and grabbed a fistful of her long, silky hair. He crouched over her, stroking her pussy like he had designed it. Tara felt faint. She wondered how many orgasms Jerome was going to wrench from her before he was through. As he hit a spot that felt so good tears that welled up in her eyes, she had a feeling it would be so many that she was going to lose count.

She would be right.

Elizabeth Rhoden poured another glass of champagne as she relaxed in the Jacuzzi in the master bedroom. It was only 11:30 a.m. Not even midday yet. Rather early to be drinking but today was a special day. A day of celebration. Her first day as a free woman. She was an escapee from the sadistic prison in which her husband had imprisoned her for the past month. Ever since that day when he had popped in the DVD of her and Jerome having sex, he had progressively taken her humiliation and degradation to a new low. The experience four nights ago had given her the courage to go through with an idea she had been toying with off and on for the past couple of years. Just thinking about what her husband had forced her to do that night made her wish that she was the one who had stabbed him in his heart.

She wanted out of the marriage but could not leave empty handed. And if she had divorced him that was exactly how she would have to leave. With nothing. She was used to living the high life, being around money. But having access to money and owning money were two entirely different things. She wanted to own money. Greed had given birth to the idea of having him killed. Self-preservation had transformed thought into action.

She was proud of herself. She had planned the bastard's murder and gotten away with it. The nosy detective had his doubts but he was nothing to be concerned about. He could stuff his doubts up his ass for all she cared. It was over. A new beginning. She was an attractive forty-five year old widow with the world at her fingertips. From this day on it was all about the pursuit of pleasure and happiness. And she had millions of dollars at her disposal to finance the journey for the rest of her life.

The last time she was this excited was when she had become his second wife twelve years ago. She sipped her champagne and smiled, appreciating the irony. She reached for the remote and turned on the TV. She scrolled to the porn channels and settled on one that was showing interracial sex. She reached down into the bubbly water and touched herself.

A quick orgasm before lunch was in order.

Lenky spent the entire morning catching up on business. It was now midday and the past few hours had been quite productive. He liaised with one of his customers in Miami and worked out a good price for him to send the guy six kilos of cocaine; met with his top soldiers and reassigned some duties and did some reshuffling; and hired a new live-in chef, a guy from his old neighbourhood who just came home from prison where he did two years for illegal possession of a firearm. He came highly recommended for his culinary skills and Lenky was always willing to help out anyone from the ghetto when he could. Besides he liked the fact that the man was a gangster. He could be given other duties other than cooking.

Lenky thought about Calvin, the fisherman from Rocky Point, as he headed to downtown Kingston where he was going to meet with a couple of cops that were on his payroll. He needed them to transport 1000 pounds of compressed marijuana from Westmoreland to Kingston safely. Some drug dealers only sold one kind of drug but Lenky didn't consider himself a drug dealer. He was an entrepreneur. He would sell shit if there was money to be made from it.

He wanted Calvin to work for him. He had been pleased to see Calvin at Mikey's funeral yesterday. Loyalty was a trait that he admired and he knew that a man like Calvin would always have his back no matter what. People like that were hard to find. All he needed to do was convince him to work for him. Be his right hand man. It wouldn't be easy. Calvin was a decent man, whose ill advised foray into criminal activities was a move of desperation to get the money for his wife's eye surgery.

But Lenky was positive that he could persuade him to come on board. He pulled over in the parking lot at Victoria Pier and parked and exited the vehicle. Blacka and Ping Pong, who had accompanied him to his rendezvous, followed him over to where the two plain clothes policemen were waiting on a bench by the waterfront.

"I met someone," Sara said, looking at Dr. Muirhead from her comfortable perch on the couch. She had kicked off her Emilio Pucci flats and her freshly groomed toes looked pretty in their bright red polish. She turned onto her side and he tried not to stare at the hint of cleavage on display and maintain eye contact. A far cry from her first visit nearly four weeks ago when the only skin visible was her face, neck and hands. "A very nice man..."

His heart sank. A million thoughts assaulted his brain at the speed of light. She had met someone. How? When? Where? Jealousy surged through his veins. He felt stupid. What was there to be jealous about? He was sixteen years her senior and she wasn't even aware of his growing affection for her. Maybe it was for the best. Then he wouldn't have to worry about crossing the patient/doctor line. Not that she would want him. She was young and beautiful, and once she was mentally healed, had her whole life ahead of her.

"I smile when I picture his face...his mannerisms... his voice soothes me...his words remind me that sometimes when the world seems to have left me in darkness, it is I that has closed my eyes."

She smiled and the room lit up. Dr. Muirhead thought that it was too soon for her to be thinking about getting involved with someone regardless of how much she liked him. The therapy was going extremely well, and getting emotionally entangled at this juncture could set her back big time. Not to mention that he didn't want her to get involved with anyone for his own personal reasons. This girl had seriously gotten under his skin. An ethical dilemma but one that he wouldn't have to deal with for very long. Based on her progress she would only need to continue seeing him for another four weeks and then she would be out of his life. The thought saddened him. *Pull yourself together Derrick.* He struggled to remain stoic and pay attention to what she was saying.

"The man I'm talking about is you..."

"Huh?" Dr. Muirhead asked, blinking stupidly. Did she just say what he thought she said?

She repeated herself, as she sat up and crossed her legs. His heart skipped two beats when he caught a glimpse of her red underwear.

Dr. Muirhead cleared his throat and removed his glasses. He had to maintain his professionalism and do the right thing.

"Sara...this is normal...I'm the person you have been sharing your most intimate thoughts with for the past three weeks...so it's only natural that you would feel some sort of affection for me but as soon your treatment is over, it will pass."

"Don't patronize me Doctor," she responded, looking at him steadily. "I know you want me too. I see it in your eyes."

Dr. Muirhead was speechless. Her progress was remarkable. In just three short weeks she was almost back to her old self. Her confidence, awareness and assertiveness were on full display. He wondered just how much of her old self would return, remembering how promiscuous she used to be.

He tried to think of an appropriate response, and couldn't, so he gave up. Sara rose and walked over to him purposefully. She went around his desk and sat on it, placing her bare feet on his thigh. His heart was pounding so hard that he swore he was going to have a heart attack.

"Sara..." he croaked. "We...I –"

She placed a manicured finger on his lips, cutting him off in midsentence.

"I know you're worried about the ethical angle of getting involved with me but it's irrelevant. I'm a big girl and I know what I want. Besides, today is our last session," she told him softly, holding onto his striped blue and white tie and pulling him towards her.

When his quivering lips were just an inch away, she kissed him.

It was the sweetest kiss he had ever had.

CHAPTER 11

"So my good friend Gunner from England is coming down tomorrow," Jerome said, sipping his wine. He was having dinner with Angela at The White Orchid, a fabulous upscale restaurant located at Hotel Soho, a small luxurious boutique hotel which added a different dimension to New Kingston. Jerome was having a boneless chicken breast stuffed with smoked ham and Swiss cheese topped with a Tarragon cream sauce, while Angela had settled for sliced sirloin topped with a brandy pepper cream sauce and lightly battered onion curls.

"Ok cool, that's the one you hung out with when you were there last month?" Angela asked, dabbing her lips delicately with the linen napkin.

Jerome nodded.

"Can't wait for you to meet him," he said. He then told her about Lenky's jealousy of his and Gunner's close friendship.

Angela found that quite amusing. She had no idea that men behaved like that.

Jerome excused himself and went to the rest room. Angela wasn't much of a drinker and he had pretty much polished off the bottle of wine by himself. He peed, flushed and washed his hands. He looked at himself in the mirror. He was wearing a fitted black Prada button down, grey True Religion jeans and black Prada loafers. Tara had brought back several outfits for him from Miami and this was one of them. *She has great taste,* Jerome mused appreciatively as he exited the bathroom and made his way back to their corner table. *Bless her heart.*

A few minutes after he rejoined Angela, he looked up as a pretty young woman and her friend approached the table. The maitre d' waited patiently a few meters away to escort them to their table when they were through.

"Hello, Jerome, nice to see you again. You're looking delicious as usual," she said, leaning over to kiss him on the cheek.

It was Marianne, the Prime Minister's niece, and one of the girls in Tara's inner circle. Jerome hadn't seen her since their rendezvous in her uncle's office at the club several weeks ago.

"Hi Marianne, good to see you. This is Angela, my girlfriend."

Marianne cocked her eyebrows.

"Angela Charlton, is that you? Wow…you snagged Jerome James? You lucky girl you…"

She laughed and leaned over to give Angela a hug. The hug was one sided.

"We went to Prep school together," Marianne explained to Jerome, seemingly oblivious to Angela's coolness towards her. "And we were in the same class at high school for three years."

Right...until they separated the smart students from the morons in the tenth grade, Angela mused.

"So...I heard you're a masseuse now?" she said, turning her attention back to Angela.

"Physiotherapist," Angela corrected tartly. "I'm sure even you can appreciate the difference."

"Hmmm ok, so how's that going for you?" Marianne asked, fussing with her hair, as if Angela's verbal jab had thrown it out of place.

"Wonderful. I have my own practice and I only take clients by appointment," Angela responded, taking a sip of her wine.

Several awkward seconds of silence ticked by, then Marianne took her leave.

"Good for you, well it was nice running into you. Bye Jerome, really nice to see you again. Take care."

"Ugh! I can't stand that bitch," Angela said when Marianne had walked off with her friend and the maitre d'. "I've disliked her since I was four years old. She's nothing but a pretentious whore who thinks that her shit can make pizza."

Jerome chuckled. He had never heard Angela speak ill of anyone. She must really hate Marianne.

"How do you know her?" Angela asked; a hint of jealousy in her pretty brown eyes. "She seemed *very* friendly towards you."

"I met her once at a party...not sure what's up with the exuberant greeting," Jerome told her, shrugging dismissively. "Maybe she was just trying to piss you off."

"Well she succeeded," Angela replied. "Signal the waiter to bring the bill. Good thing I've already eaten or she would have surely spoiled my appetite."

"What happen to yuh forehead?" Lenky asked, when Jada came into the living room. He had just gotten back to Kingston from Portmore where he had gone to look at a commercial building that was for sale, and decided to stop by and pay his son and Jada a visit.

"Mi drop and hit it," Jada told him, as she came over to give him a hug. She had no idea why the damn lump was taking so long to go down. A constant reminder of her embarrassment at the hands of her nemesis. She had not left the house since it happened other than to go to the funeral. She was very self conscious about it.

"Yuh hit your head hard J," he said, examining the offending lump, trying not to laugh.

"Yeah, I hit it on the edge of the face basin," she explained. Obviously neither Blacka nor that bitch Laura had mentioned the fight to Lenky; which was great as he would have surely given her a beating for fighting his pregnant wife.

Lenky then sat on the carpet and played a videogame with his son for several minutes, much to Nathaniel's delight. Jada watched them with a wistful smile. This was how it should be. All three of them living together – in Lenky's mansion of course, not here in the ghetto – as one happy family. Lenky had ejaculated in her twice on his last visit. Her period was due next week and she was praying that it would be late. She wanted to give him a daughter in the worst way. She was convinced that it was one of the keys in reclaiming her number one spot.

After his son beat him in the violent *God of War 11,* Lenky gave Jada fifty thousand dollars to pay for Nathaniel's summer camp and to get him some new gear. He'd be damned if he was going to allow him to stay home playing videogames all summer. The boy needed some exercise. He was already too chubby. Lenky slapped Jada on the ass playfully and made his way outside where Blacka and Ping Pong were holding court with some young thugs from the community. Lenky gave the youths some money and the trio left. It had been a long, busy and productive day. Lenky felt contented as he reclined in the passenger seat and lit the marijuana joint that Ping Pong had rolled for him.

It was the best he was feeling since the day he received the phone call that Mikey was dead.

"Ohhhh baby...mmmm...that feels so good...mmmm..." Angela moaned as she clutched the sheets tightly. Jerome's head was between her legs, trying and succeeding, to drain her body of its nutrients. Long gone was her anger at Marianne's comments and hypocrisy at the restaurant. Jerome had licked and sucked them away, turning her into a quivering mass of flesh in the process. He had her pussy open like a hibiscus flower in full bloom. His thumbs held her lips apart, giving him full access to her sweet essence. It was hard to believe that Jerome had never eaten pussy before her. His tongue was as dexterous as his magnificent dick. She could feel her climax slowly marching towards her center, inched along gently with each flick of his tongue against her rock hard clit.

"Yes...yes...Jerome...I'm almost there baby...don't stop...almost...there...oh God..."

Her climax was now steadily approaching, picking up pace, surging towards the finish line.

Jerome's tongue was moving at the speed of light, whipping her pussy into a frenzy. Angela stiffened and held Jerome's head in place as she squirted into his mouth. Jerome groaned as he reveled in her explosion, the loud slurping sounds he was making as he lapped up her sweet stickiness providing the background effects for her soulful moans and his animal-like groans.

When Angela caught her breath, Jerome led them over to the large bedroom window. It was open, and the curtains floated around their bodies like erotic ghosts as Angela held on to the window sill and bent over slightly. She looked at the trees swaying in the brisk breeze as Jerome entered her from behind.

She soared with each stroke, and by her third orgasm the trees seemed like they were far away, far below her.

CHAPTER 12

Gunner sauntered towards the exit with the porter and his Louis Vuitton luggage set in tow. He had arrived on the first flight in to Jamaica from Heathrow, and after a brief hassle with customs over the amount of clothing he brought with him for a ten day visit, which ended once he told them that he was Jerome James' half brother and slipped the officer a hundred pound note, he was now ready to enjoy his vacation. Jerome was supposed to be outside waiting for him.

He spotted Jerome immediately. Jerome was surrounded by airport workers, visitors, and a couple of police officers, all anxious to get a word in with the talented, popular football star.

"Jerome!" Gunner called out, stopping a few meters away. Jerome looked over, excused himself from his group of admirers and made his way over to Gunner, grinning broadly.

They gave each other a manly half-hug and Jerome directed the porter to the black Mercedes SUV that was parked illegally by the curb. This area was designated only for pick-ups, not parking, and it was strictly enforced by airport security personnel but Jerome was an exception.

"Nice...this will do," Gunner commented as he climbed into the passenger seat. He had rented the vehicle for the duration of his stay and had made arrangements for it to be taken to Jerome's home this morning. Jerome had told him that transportation wouldn't be a problem as he had full use of Lenky's Lexus jeep, but Gunner would have no part of that. He had firmly told Jerome that he wouldn't be riding around in any of Lenky's vehicles. He could rent his own.

"I thought you were going to bring Deborah," Jerome commented as he overtook a line of vehicles on the Palisadoes Road.

"Yeah, but then I reckoned why bring sand to the beach," Gunner quipped. "Besides after what happened to Sara she wouldn't have any female friends to hang with whenever you and I want to go out alone. And I don't need her all up on me 24/7 for my entire vacation. I just want to have some fun and chill. I'm not even conducting any business on this trip. She'll be ok."

Jerome chuckled.

When they got into Kingston, Jerome went straight to the Barcelona Court, Kingston's most expensive hotel, where Gunner had booked one of the two Presidential suites for the duration of his stay.

The pretty receptionist that Gunner was dealing with at the front desk was clearly taken by him despite her efforts to maintain her professionalism. Her eyes had casually taken in his Mardi Gras beads-esque platinum chain, his diamond encrusted Philippe Patek watch and his tall wiry frame clad in a brown army style Dior shirt and fitted Marc Jacobs jeans, his handsome face draped by Cartier shades and looked away suitably impressed.

"Enjoy your stay with us, Mr. Burke," she said as she handed him back his black card and his room key, her eyes twinkling through her smart prescription lenses.

He grazed her fingers intentionally as he took the card and key from her.

"Thanks, I definitely intend to. 846-7777," he responded, and walked away after staring her down for several seconds. He was willing to bet his life that those numbers were etched in her memory. At least until she wrote it down.

He then took the elevator up with the porter and his luggage while Jerome remained in the lobby where they had a coffee and pastry shop. Jerome had a latte and chatted with a businessman who recognized him while he waited for Gunner. It was a fortuitous meeting. The man was a vice president at Nike with responsibility for Latin America and the Caribbean. He was very interested in having discussions with Jerome regarding an endorsement deal. He had been monitoring Jerome's career since his jaw-dropping performance in Jamaica's crucial world cup qualifying game against Mexico a few months ago and had planned to contact him soon. Meeting him unexpectedly in the hotel lobby had only hastened the contact.

Jerome sipped his latte and tried to be cool though he was very excited at the prospect of a Nike endorsement deal. He did not yet have an official agent, the Jamaica Football Association boss usually helped him with decisions like this but as he got bigger, which was inevitable, he would probably sign with a sports agent to maximize his earnings on and off the field. But for now he was sure that he could handle his business.

He listened as the man, Victor Silvera, told him that he would be willing to sign him to a three year deal valued at five hundred thousand pounds. Jerome smiled inwardly. The three year offer was no coincidence. The man obviously knew that Jerome's deal with Manchester FC was a three year one. He was only willing to commit to the three years that he was certain that Jerome would be at a highly visible club. Jerome had no problem with that but he wanted more money. He was confident that by the end of his first season he would be an international star.

"Tell you what," Jerome began. "Six hundred thousand pounds guaranteed for the three years whether I get injured or dropped from the team or any other unlikely scenario, and a five thousand pound sponsorship bonus for every goal I score."

Silvera was silent for a few moments. Clearly he had expected Jerome to jump at the offer and not counter with one of his own. He looked at Jerome steadily before responding. Jerome merely sipped his latte and held his gaze.

Then Silvera smiled ruefully and extended his beefy hand.

"You have a deal, Jerome," he said. "My lawyer at the London office will draw up the papers and contact you when you arrive in England."

Jerome grinned and shook his hand firmly.

"Looking forward to hearing from him, and thank you, you made a good decision."

Silvera laughed.

"Let's hope so."

Gunner returned from upstairs, having showered and changed into a Dior T-shirt, an unbuttoned vest, distressed True Religion jeans and Paul Smith trainers. Silvera gave Jerome his business card and told him that they would be in touch.

Jerome and Gunner then made their way outside. The pretty receptionist watched them until they were out of sight.

Laura sighed with frustration. She had been calling Jerome since yesterday and left several messages on his voicemail. He had yet to return her calls. She was at the poolside lounging with a novel but she could not concentrate. She was still furious with him for having sex at her home with that bitch he was with the night of the wake. She needed to vent. She dialed his number again, planning to leave another scathing message but to her surprise he picked up on the third ring.

"Jerome is this how you're treating me now? Ignoring my calls?" she asked icily.

"Actually I missed the first two first calls because I was in the bathroom but after hearing your feisty messages I decided not to call back...you need some time to cool off."

"Fuck you! Why did you disrespect me like that the other night? Huh? You-"

She almost threw the phone into the pool when she realized that he had hung up on her. She wanted a drink so badly but couldn't because of the baby. The baby that she needed to get rid of before it was too late. And she needed Jerome's help to do it. She was so angry and frustrated that she was shaking.

Nothing seemed to be going right.

"You good mate?" Gunner asked, from his relaxed perch on the passenger seat.

"Yeah man, all is well," Jerome responded as he headed down Hagley Park road. They were on their way to Hellshire beach. Gunner was dying to have some of the steam fish and lobster that the beach was famous for. Jerome did not elaborate as he had not told Gunner that he was sleeping with Lenky's wife. Some secrets were too deadly to be shared.

Gunner's mobile rang as Jerome entered the toll road leading to Portmore.

"Hello," he said, lighting a cigarette and putting the window down. Smoking is like a hiccup. You light one near a smoker and they're going to want one too. Jerome lit up as well, turned off the air conditioner and lowered his window.

"Hi, is this Damon Burke?" a softly accented voice asked.

Gunner smiled. It was the receptionist from the hotel.

"It is...hello beautiful..."

She chuckled.

"How'd you know it was me?"

"Well apart from recognizing that sexy voice of yours...you're the only person who could possibly call me on this phone and use my government name."

She chuckled again.

"I see...what name would they use?"

"Gunner. What's yours...or do I keep calling you beautiful?"

"Gunner huh? Sounds dangerous...my name is Lola...Lola Lopez."

"Nice...you're a Latina," Gunner said; flicking ash into the wind as Jerome switched lanes, blowing past slower moving vehicles. "Are you off work yet?"

"Yes, Cuban. I just got off...I'm waiting on a cab now to go home," she told him.

"I want to see you...take the cab home, change quickly and then take the cab over to Hellshire beach and call me when you get there. I'll pay for everything."

A take charge kind of guy. Lola liked that. She told him that she would and ended the call.

"Not wasting any time are we?" Jerome teased.

Gunner grinned.

"Nope...time is money and money is pussy."

Jerome laughed. He liked that.

That was a good one.

As usual, there was a decent sized crowd at the beach. Lots of scantily clad women of all shapes and sizes were lounging, eating or swimming while men sat around watching them. Children were also in the mix, running around, playing in their own world. Jerome led Gunner over to Reds' restaurant shack. Reds had the best fish on the beach. His face lit up like a hundred watt bulb when he saw his famous customer.

"Jerome! What ah gwaan?" he exclaimed, giving Jerome a hearty handshake.

"What's up Reds...I brought you a new customer. This is Gunner, my good friend from England."

Reds shook Gunner's hand.

"Respect, British," he said.

Gunner nodded.

They sat on one of the wooden benches at the front of Reds' humble establishment and Jerome beckoned to a guy that he knew sold good marijuana. He purchased five hundred dollars worth and he and Gunner rolled two joints. They ordered a bottle of Hennessy and a bottle of cranberry juice from a nearby bar, and people-watched as they enjoyed the potent weed and liquor while Reds prepared their order.

The food was made to order, and it would be at least forty-five minutes to an hour before it was ready. That suited Gunner just fine as he didn't want Lola's food to be cold.

Jerome's phone rang in the middle of an earnest conversation about football with some fans that had drifted over to have a few words with their hero. It was Lenky.

"So because your big friend come down mi nuh hear from yuh from morning," Lenky teased, though Jerome knew that he was serious.

"Nah...nothing like that," Jerome said easily. "We're just on the beach chilling and getting some fish. Remember that we're all going to link up at the club later."

Tuesday night was 'ladies night' at Krave, a new nightclub on Kingston's hip strip and they had planned to go there for the first time tonight. It had opened the day after Mikey's death so they hadn't had a chance to check it out yet.

"Yeah man, I still plan to go," Lenky concurred.

"Oh, you can send for the Lexus later. Gunner rented a vehicle and seeing as he doesn't like driving out here, the Lexus would just be parked at my house for the next week and a half, so if you need it send for it," Jerome told him.

Jerome then asked him if he wanted to speak to Gunner but Lenky declined, saying that he'll see them later. When Jerome hung up there was a text message from Laura:

Jerome I'm sorry. I was just really jealous. I apologize for the nasty messages I left on your voicemail. Please call me tomorrow about midday. We need to talk. I love you.

Ps. And I'm horny. I need you inside me.

Jerome shook his head and slipped the phone inside his pocket. At least she had come to her senses.

Gunner was just coming off his phone.

"Lola is here…she already paid for the cab and is walking in, let's go meet her."

They were about to get up when they saw her approaching. Every male who saw her, and quite a few females, were staring. She strutted nonchalantly towards them, oblivious or indifferent to the attention that she was getting. Her almost waist length hair, which earlier had been severely pulled back in a tight bun, was now free to revel in the sea breeze. Her reading glasses had been replaced by oversized sunglasses and her body, hidden behind the desk at the hotel, was now on full display. Her long legs were spilling out of tiny denim shorts and her firm, ridiculously pert breasts, were rebelling against the fabric of her tank top.

"Damn..." Gunner muttered, smiling like a man that had just won the lottery.

Jerome nodded approvingly. Gunner had lucked out indeed. The Latina was truly one hot specimen.

"Hi Gunner," she said as she walked up to him and hugged him.

"Hey sexy," he responded, giving her a quick peck on her lip-gloss coated lips.

She smiled at Jerome and waved hi.

Jerome was amazed at the instant chemistry between them. No one could ever have guessed that they had met a mere two hours ago with limited interaction.

"That was quick," Gunner commented as they all sat down on the bench.

"I was anxious to see you...besides I don't generally take long to get ready."

Her smile stirred something deep inside Gunner. He was really, really feeling her and he knew nothing about her. He knew right then and there that she was going to be his woman. If that wasn't crazier than a soup sandwich he didn't know what was.

Reds finally served their food and it was well worth the wait. Fried lobster with butter and garlic sauce, steamed parrot and snapper fish served 'soupy' style with crackers and festival. The trio dug in with gusto. The food was absolutely delicious. A prelude to what Gunner was certain would be a very interesting night.

His trip was off to a brilliant start.

CHAPTER 13

The ride back into Kingston was filled with sexual tension. So much so that it felt like six people were in the vehicle as opposed to three. They had all had a good time, eating, drinking, chatting, and in the case of Gunner and Lola, constant touching and flirting. The original plan had been to take Gunner to meet Angela after leaving the beach but that would have to be done tomorrow.

Jerome pulled up at the Barcelona Court hotel and stopped in front of the entrance. Lola suddenly looked disturbed.

"Oh shit Papi...it's against the rules for employees to fraternize with the guests at the hotel...I can't be seen going to your suite," she said, her voice trembling with disappointment.

Gunner waved his hand dismissively.

"Well tender your resignation tomorrow...there's no way you're not coming up with me now. Don't worry, we'll sort everything out. Money will be the least of your problems. Fuck this job."

Lola smiled and shook her head as she exited the vehicle. *I must be loco*, she mused as Gunner held her hand and marched right into the lobby after telling Jerome to call him later and let him know what time he would be picking them up to go clubbing.

The security guard on duty in the lobby knew Lola and watched with wide, envious eyes as she went into an elevator with the man, who was obviously a guest. He noted that they were going to the 12th floor. Only the two Presidential suites were up there. He had heard several men in the lunch room talk about Lola. They all wanted to fuck her but she never gave anyone the time of day, not even any of the hotel executives. And now here she was breaking company rules openly like she owned shares in the hotel. He went over to the night manager's office to report her.

"Mmmmm...damn...baby..." Angela moaned as Jerome bent her over right by the front door and ate her out from behind as he stroked his shaft, which was jutting angrily from the fly of his jeans. He had pounced on her the second he had entered the apartment. They were both still fully dressed, her panties and shorts were pulled down mid thigh and her baby T was pushed up over her breasts. She had no idea what had gotten into him but she wasn't complaining.

She had expected him to bring his friend to meet her; instead she was being treated to some I-want-you-so-fucking-badly-sex.

"Ohhhhhh...Jesus Christ!" she blasphemed when his dick replaced his tongue inside her. She bent over some more and pushed her shorts and panties down until they slipped to her ankles. She then shook one leg free and assumed a wide legged stance to better accommodate him. She knew that she was in for a rough ride. His dick felt like a large piece of sugar coated steel. It was so *hard*. And felt so *good*.

It was impossible to get used to Jerome's love-making. It was always ridiculously intense. And the intensity seemed to be greater each time.

"Baby! Baby! Oh my God! I'm coming already!"

Her legs trembled and her heart pounded as she climaxed hard, drenching his dick with her juices. Jerome swung one leg onto the arm of the sofa and really got down to business.

"Whose pussy?" he growled, holding on to her hips tightly as he made her wail like a banshee with each impossibly deep stroke.

"Yours baby! Yours! Oh God!" Angela wailed, wondering and not caring if the neighbours could hear her. Her man was fucking her into tomorrow and she didn't care if the world knew.

"Tell me how my dick feels," Jerome commanded, as he slowed his pace and started to rotate his waistline, grinding into her wetness deeply and slowly, eliciting melodic moans from deep inside Angela's soul.

"Mmmm...baby...fuck...sweet Jesus...you're gonna make me come again...mmmm...it feels like heaven ...feels...so good...so fucking good...I'm coming...I love you...coming again...I love you baby...ahhhh...ohhhhhh..."

Jerome pulled out of her and she slumped against the arm of the sofa, her energy temporarily sapped, drained by her intense orgasms.

"Oh baby...damn...I feel intoxicated..."

Jerome laughed.

"Some of the Hennessy must have seeped out," he joked.

Angela chuckled and reached for his still rigid shaft. She ran her thumb over the slit.

"Mmmm...seems like Hennessy wasn't the only thing seeping out...come here baby...come let me finish you off."

Angela got down on the carpet and laid on her back.

"Fuck me baby...come and give me all of that juice... give it to me baby..."

Jerome joined her on the carpet and did just that.

CHAPTER 14

"We need to go and shower...Jerome will be here to pick us up in an hour and we'll have to stop by your place so that you can get dressed," Gunner said to Lola, as he ran his hands through her silky hair.

"Yeah..." she sighed contentedly, snuggling up against his rock hard body even tighter. Her head was on his chest, and one leg was draped over him, his dick touching the back of her thigh, a reminder of the pleasures that she had just experienced.

They were in the queen sized bed relaxing after a torrid love making session that had concluded on the balcony, looking out at the New Kingston metropolis. Kingston was a breathtaking view at night, but not as breathtaking as the primal, passionate and vocal sex that the two new lovebirds had just had.

Gunner was in a thoughtful mood. He had heard of love at first sight – even Jerome had confided that he had fallen for Angela the first time he laid eyes on her – but he had never expected in a million years to experience it for himself. Yet here he was, totally blown away by the Latina in his arms. Cupid had ambushed him. Shot him in the back, catching him off guard. He was used to liking one girl more than others but this bubbly, fluttering, mushy feeling in his insides was an alien concept.

He was sophisticated enough to know that just because she had slept with him so quickly did not mean that she was a slut, that this was something she did all the time. He had quieted her fears about that with reassuring kisses. They had a special connection. One that defied rules and logic.

He checked the time and they reluctantly crawled out of bed and went into the bathroom to shower.

The hip strip was bursting at the seams with activity. Posh cars were cruising on the strip profiling, lots of people were milling about on either side of the strip and the line to get into Krave extended all the way down to the Western Union branch at the end of the block. Lenky, who arrived a few minutes before Jerome, was given the last available parking spot in front of the club by one of the security guards who recognized him the minute he pulled up. He stepped out of the vehicle dressed in full black, his eyes hidden behind Prada shades. With him were Ping Pong, Blacka, and three attractive, voluptuous young ladies.

He was just about to call Jerome when a black Mercedes SUV pulled up next to his Lincoln Navigator.

"What's up Lenky?" Jerome said, after he lowered the window. He put the vehicle in park and stepped out. People stared, as Jerome, clad in a tan blazer and Gucci loafers, greeted Lenky warmly.

Gunner, dressed in full white down to his Dior shades, exited the vehicle with Lola in tow. She looked beautiful in her strapless red dress and six inch black and red stilettos.

"Lenky...what's up mate?" he said, as he greeted Lenky with a firm handshake.

"Yes Gunner," Lenky responded coolly, trying not to stare at Gunner's exquisitely designed platinum chain. "Good to see you."

"This is Lola," Gunner said, by way of introduction.

"Nice to meet the lovely lady...it's Valentine's Day?" Lenky quipped, referring to the couple's red and white ensemble.

"For us it is...love is in the air," Gunner responded easily.

Lola merely treated Lenky to a polite smile. She disliked him on sight.

Ready to go inside the club and get the party started, Jerome called over one of the security guys that he knew and handed him the keys to the rented Mercedes.

"Park this and hold on to the keys until I'm ready," Jerome told him, slipping him a thousand dollar bill. "Buy yourself a drink."

The security guard thanked him profusely and Jerome and the entourage made their way inside through the VIP entrance. They did not pay to go in. They headed straight to VIP and took over two of the couches and the corresponding table. One of the waitresses, dressed in a cute, skimpy white outfit, came over immediately to take their order.

"I'll get the first round," Lenky announced.

"Nah mate, I got it," Gunner said, and before Lenky could protest, told the young lady to bring four bottles of Hennessey and six bottles of the best champagne along with twelve cans of red bull and six bottles of cranberry juice. He handed her his black card.

Lenky, seated amongst the three women whom he had taken to the club, was visibly annoyed.

"Yo Gunner...why you do that? I said the first round was on me," he complained.

Gunner, who was slouched on the couch with his legs crossed, lit a cigarette before responding.

"Its not a big deal mate, you can get the next round," he responded after taking a deep drag.

Everyone knew that the amount of liquor he had ordered would not be finished tonight. Another round would not be needed.

Lenky was not amused. He felt like Gunner was trying to show him up. But he decided to play it cool. No sense in allowing this to spoil the night. But Gunner had better chill the fuck out. This wasn't England.

First Gunner was trying to come between him and Jerome; then slighted him by renting a vehicle though he knew that he had lots of luxury vehicles at his disposal, and now this. Lenky accepted the marijuana joint that Ping Pong had rolled for him and lit it. Marijuana smoking was not allowed in the club but no one, not even the three security personnel stationed in the VIP area batted an eye.

Yeah...ah my world this, Lenky mused, as the potent weed calmed him. *Gunner need to know that. Before mi have to teach him a lesson.*

After three soft, unanswered knocks, the door to Sara's bedroom opened. The figure in the doorway loomed on the wall like a poltergeist. Sara was awake, but remained still and pretended to be asleep. She knew that it was her dad. He entered the room and walked over to the bed, his steps muted by the plush white carpet. Everything in the room was new, in honor of her returning home, as though being surrounded by pretty new things would have helped her to get over the vicious rape.

He stood and looked at his daughter's sleeping form. Sara wondered for a brief second if he was going to attempt what he had not done since she was sixteen. That was the last time he had molested her. The last time she had allowed him to touch her.

Shortly after that she bought home her first real boyfriend to introduce to the family. At that time she was beginning to break free of his sick brainwashing. Her eyes had opened to the fact that what he had been doing to her since the tender age of eight was terribly wrong. A horrible act against an innocent child that worshipped him, loved him, and wanted to please him in every way.

Daddy's little girl indeed. But everything changed when she bit the apple of reality and feeling special and loved, were replaced by burdensome shame and guilt, emotions so intense and crippling that she was sometimes unable to function. They took hold of her fragile, distorted sixteen year old brain and forced her to wake up and put an end to the insane depravity.

He began to treat her like an unwanted stepchild, and when her frustration at having to keep every-thing inside began to manifest itself in promiscuity, self-loathing and aimlessness, he pretended not to know the root cause and turned his back on her; left her to self-destruct.

Precious Angela became his favourite, and was treated like a princess, without having to do anything for it. Why her, she had always wondered. Why was she the one singled out for abuse? She had never had the courage to ask him, as bringing it up would have forced her to face her own demons. *Why didn't you tell your mother the first time it happened? Why did you allow it to go on for eight years? Progress from touching to full blown sex? Admit it, you liked it.*

The voices were relentless, quick to choke her with a necklace of guilt and a medallion of shame, quick to convince her that she was not blameless, and was also at fault, that she had done something wrong.

But good things can come out of the most heinous circumstances. She had met Derrick, bless his heart. His compassion and kindness, his genuine liking for her, his wisdom and understanding, had given her a lifeline and was pulling her up bit by bit from the emotional cesspool in which she had been drowning. She was well on her way to conquering her demons. The wounds would leave terrible scars, but they would be healed.

Derrick was the only person on earth that she had ever spoken to about the sexual and emotional abuse she had suffered at the hands of her dad. She had told him three evenings ago, as they enjoyed a quiet dinner at his apartment.

No one knew of their budding romance. They were taking things slow, an alien concept to her, but one she needed to learn, to experience. They had gone no further than several passionate kisses. It was a task for her to restrain herself. All her life she had sought love by opening her legs, now she was learning that she had so much more to offer.

Her whole was much more than the sum of her parts.

Her father left her bedroom and closed the door quietly behind him.

The rich, prominent David Charlton.

An upstanding member of Jamaican society.

If only the world knew the kind of man that he really was.

If only the world could see him without his mask.

Jerome and the entourage exited the club at 4 a.m. Everyone had a good time though it was obvious that there was some tension between Gunner and Lenky, especially from Lenky's end. Jerome didn't like it but what could he do. They were both his good friends, had known each other as business acquaintances before they met him, but now Lenky had a bug up his ass because he and Gunner were now close friends.

Lenky was of the impression that Gunner was acting like he had more money than anybody else and tried to show him up every chance he got. He wasn't going to put up with it and the next time

Gunner tried to pull another stunt, he was going to discipline him. Jerome had nodded gravely, as Lenky told him all of this while both of them had stood alone to one side watching the three girls that Lenky brought to the club dance seductively with each other. Jerome thought Lenky was overreacting and making much ado about nothing, and that the situation was getting out of hand but he didn't bother to say anything.

Gunner would only be in Jamaica for nine more days. Hopefully there would not be a confrontation with him getting caught in the middle. But he would speak to Gunner about it. It was only right that he knew how deep Lenky's animosity ran towards him. They descended the steps, everyone quite tipsy, and the security guard that had parked the vehicle for Jerome hurried to fetch it. Everyone said their goodbyes and the two parties left in their separate vehicles.

Jerome told Gunner what Lenky said on the ride to the hotel. Lola was very tipsy, almost asleep on the back seat. Gunner listened and chuckled. He wasn't alarmed in the least.

"Lenky is just jealous and envious...female traits," Gunner said dismissively. "Discipline me? Lenky is a real funny bloke. Picture that with a Kodak. Don't worry yourself Jerome, Lenky can't do shit to me."

They arrived at the hotel and Jerome drove off, promising to pick him up at 1 p.m. in the afternoon. Jerome thought about Gunner's response to Lenky's indirect threat. He hoped that Gunner wasn't under-estimating Lenky. This was Lenky's turf, and he had killers at his beck and call, even legal ones in uniform. Jerome whipped out his mobile and called Dimples. It was now 4:30 a.m.

She answered on the fourth ring.

"Hey baby...you alright?" she said through a yawn.

"Nope...I'm horny," Jerome told her. "I'm coming to pick you up now."

Dimples chuckled. She was instantly wide awake. She hadn't seen him in over three weeks and that was three weeks too long. He must have been out partying and was now under the influence. Sex with Jerome was always off the chain, but a tipsy Jerome? She was in for a serious pounding. She was so excited that she swore her pussy had already gone ahead to the bathroom to take a shower.

"Ok baby," Dimples responded, as she threw the covers aside and got up.

"Is who that?" the figure in the bed next to her queried, turning his head to look at her in the semi-darkness.

"None of your damn business," Dimples responded matter-of-factly over her shoulder as she exited the bedroom. Dougie, the guy in her bed, was ten years her junior and her current boy toy of the moment. He had no say in anything. His job was only to give her sex when she needed it, not to act like he was her man. He didn't work yet he wore the latest clothes and always had money in his pocket, courtesy of her. What more could he want?

She got inside the bathroom, took off her T-shirt and climbed into the shower, her massive breasts swinging with her movements. She showered quickly, not wanting Jerome to arrive and she wasn't ready to go.

CHAPTER 15

Jerome went by the hotel at 1:15 p.m. to pick up Gunner and Lola after dropping home Dimples. He parked by the curb close to the front of the lobby, illegally allowed to do so by the security guard who was a huge fan of his. Gunner was sitting in the lobby conversing with four strange men. Jerome went over there just as the men were getting up.

"What's up mate," Gunner said, giving him a pound.

"Chilling bro," Jerome responded, wondering who these guys were. "Everything good?"

"Yep...this is my boy Bishop and his crew from Rockfort. They'll be hanging with us every now and then for the rest of my stay."

Jerome now understood. They were Gunner's gangster associates who would be around to deal with any problems that might arise from Lenky. Jerome had heard of Bishop but had never seen him. He looked nothing like one would expect a cold-blooded killer to look. He had gentle eyes, an easy going manner and was very soft spoken. He was the leader of a notorious gang based in Rockfort that had made the news on many occasions. Bishop was a wanted man. Jerome could only surmise that not many people knew what he looked like, including the police who were looking for him.

Jerome didn't like this development as it hammered home the fact that things could easily get dangerous between his two friends. Somebody could get killed. And for what? Petty jealousy. But he understood that Gunner had to take Lenky's threat seriously and be ready for whatever.

The four men all knew who Jerome was and they congratulated him on his contract with the British club. They then took their leave.

"So where's Lola?" Jerome asked.

"She's gone to her boss' office to tender her resignation," Gunner told him.

"Oh I had carried some stuff for you, let's go get them in the meantime," Gunner suggested.

Jerome nodded and they headed towards the elevator. They stopped when they saw Lola storming towards them. A security guard was behind her.

"Stop! The boss said he's not finished!" the man said forcefully, though he was attempting to keep his voice down, so as not to cause a scene in the lobby. Too late, people were already staring.

He grabbed Lola by the shoulder. She turned around and slapped him in the face. Gunner and Jerome rushed over there. Gunner grabbed the security guard before he could touch Lola again and punched him in the face. The guy toppled to the ground and three other security personnel rushed over.

"What is going on here?" one of them asked. He was wearing a different colour shirt from the others, apparently he was their supervisor.

Before anyone could respond, Lola's boss, a handsome, tall, barrel-chested man with a receding hairline, came out through a door labeled Human Resources and strode purposefully over towards them.

"Burford! Escort Miss Lopez off the premises immediately," he barked at the security officer in the grey shirt; his face red with embarrassment at what was taking in place in full view of some of the guests. This was a five star hotel, not some hole in the wall.

"Like hell he will," Gunner said, stepping to Lola's boss. "If your security detail touches her there'll be hell to pay. Miss Lopez is with me."

"And who are you?" the man challenged.

"I'm a guest here, occupant of one of the Presidential Suites. Lola is my wife and she's staying here with me. Is there a fucking problem?"

The man's eyes registered surprise and his nostrils flared with anger. He swallowed and offered a conciliatory smile that did not reach his eyes. He extended a hand to Gunner.

"I'm sorry Mr. –" he prompted.

"Burke," Gunner responded; ignoring the man's outstretched hand.

"I'm her boss, I mean former boss, and apparently there has been some misunderstanding –"

Gunner stopped him in mid-sentence.

"There is no misunderstanding. She has quit this shitty job and she's staying in my suite. After I leave she'll never set foot in this hotel again. End of story."

The man was so angry that a vein in his forehead seemed to be getting more pronounced with each passing second.

"She won't be able to get a good recommendation from us when she seeks another job under the circumstances," he seethed, adjusting the lapels of his jacket.

Gunner chuckled derisively.

"She doesn't have to work another day in her life if she doesn't want to. Fuck a recommendation. I'm rich."

With that he threw his arm around Lola and walked off. Jerome followed, chuckling in amusement. It was great having Gunner around. Never a dull moment.

They headed out to the vehicle instead of going up to the suite. Jerome could collect the things that Gunner had bought for him later.

They had stuff to do on the road.

After dropping off Gunner and Lola at one of the malls in Half-Way-Tree so that Gunner could take Lola shopping, Jerome headed up to a plaza off Constant Spring Road where Laura was getting her hair done. Jerome pulled up in a vacant spot in the parking lot and called her.

"I'm outside," he said without preamble and hung up.

A few minutes later, he saw Laura come into the parking lot, looking around for Lenky's SUV that Jerome usually drove. He called her on the phone and told her that he was in the black Mercedes SUV to her right. Looking surprised, she walked over and got inside the vehicle.

She smiled and hugged him tightly.

"I missed you baby...and I'm so sorry for my behaviour...but you know it's because I love you so much...right?"

"You have to learn to watch your mouth Laura... you can't just say stuff like that to me because you're angry. If you ever disrespect me like that again I'm going to cut you off," Jerome told her, trying to ignore his growing erection. Laura's nearness was having its usual effect on him. Her head was resting on his shoulder and he could feel her breath on his nape. Her full breasts, even fuller now due to her pregnancy were calling his name, begging him to suck and caress them.

Laura's heart stopped at his words.

"No baby, please don't say that...oh my God...I can't imagine not having you in my life. I know it's just a piece of you but it means the world to me...you mean the world to me...I'm sorry baby...it won't happen again..."

Her lips reached up and claimed his. She moaned in his mouth as she kissed him hungrily, longingly, devouring his lips and tongue in a passionate frenzy.

She sighed in frustration when she came up for air.

"I want you now baby...fuck...feel how wet I am..."

Jerome slipped his hand underneath her Chloe summer dress. He didn't even have to shift her panties to find out. Her thong was soaked.

"Today looks kinda sticky...but try and get away tomorrow for a couple of hours," Jerome told her.

Laura massaged his dick through his jeans and sighed again.

"Ok baby...is this yours...I like it," she said, referring to the SUV.

"Nah, my friend is visiting from London and he rented it."

"Oh ok...Lenky doesn't like your friend...I heard him talking about him earlier today. Did something happen at the club last night?" Laura asked, still softly massaging his crotch.

"Not really...just a minor thing," Jerome responded.

"It didn't seem that way but whatever," Laura said, wondering if she should take out Jerome's dick and give him a quick blowjob.

"So...what are you going to do about the pregnancy?" Jerome asked.

Laura forgot about the blowjob and straightened up in her seat.

"I have to terminate it Jerome...I can't take the chance. If the baby is born and looks like you Lenky would kill me, you and the baby."

Jerome nodded slowly. She was quite right. Lenky would lose his damn mind. He would be away in England plying his trade but that didn't mean that Lenky couldn't put a hit out on him. It was simply too risky. There was no way around it. Laura had to have an abortion.

"I'll make the arrangements babe...soon."

Laura hugged him, feeling a huge burden being lifted off her shoulders. Jerome would take care of it and they would get pass this. Potential tragedy would be averted. She sighed. She couldn't wait for her life to get back to normal. She didn't want to have any children. At least not right now. Especially if it wasn't for Jerome.

Ten minutes later, after Laura exited the vehicle, he decided to give Elizabeth Rhoden a call.

"Well, well...if it isn't the prodigal stud," she quipped.

Jerome chuckled. It was the first time he was speaking to her since he told in no uncertain terms to leave him alone several weeks ago.

"I heard about your husband...my deepest condolences for your loss," Jerome responded. "How are you keeping up?"

"Thank you my dear...it was quite a traumatic experience but I'm keeping up rather well under the circumstances."

"That's good to hear," Jerome responded. "If there's anything I can do let me know."

"Actually there is...if you're not very busy could I swing by your apartment? Death makes me very horny."

Jerome was surprised. The woman's husband had been brutally murdered in front of her a few nights ago yet here she was requesting dick. Jerome shook his head in wonder. But to each his own, and he wasn't a judgemental person. Besides he was a bit horny himself. Laura had gotten him worked up.

"Let me check on something and call you right back," Jerome told her.

"Ok, please do."

Jerome called Gunner to see if they were ready to be picked up. Gunner told him to go ahead and do his thing as Lola was still shopping and afterwards they were going to get a bite to eat at one of the restaurants in the vicinity.

Jerome called Elizabeth back and told her to meet him at his apartment in fifteen minutes.

Detective Corporal Spence smiled when he saw the black SLK Mercedes coupe exit the Rhoden home. He gunned his engine and followed at a discreet distance. He had been staking out the Rhoden home whenever he had the time since his talk with Elizabeth Rhoden. He didn't know what he hoped to find out or accomplish by this unauthorized stakeout but the case was bothering him too much. He just had to know if his hunch was correct. She had only left the house once as far as he knew, and that was on Monday in the presence of her attorney. He had taken her down to the funeral home and then they had spent some time at his office. But today she was all alone in the sports car. Didn't use the family limo and driver. His instinct told him that she was up to something. He lit a cigarette and followed her onto Constant Spring road.

Gunner smiled as he watched Lola model the latest outfit that she had picked out. They had been shopping for over an hour and a half but he didn't mind. He was having a great time. He liked being around her so much he suspected that he could enjoy watching paint dry as long as she was watching with him. He gave her two thumbs up for the leggings, stilettos and trendy jacket that she had put together. Though she was well aware that money was no object, he noticed that she didn't select her pieces by brand, or by price. As long it looked good on her, she would rock it. And she looked good in damn near anything. He liked that. She smiled, pleased that he liked it, and went back inside the dressing room. The store attendant who was assisting Lola sighed inwardly as she put the pieces that Lola didn't want back on the racks.

Why couldn't she find a nice, handsome man to spend money on her like this? Some girls had all the luck.

Elizabeth Rhoden pulled up behind the Mercedes SUV parked in front of Jerome's apartment. She slipped her phone back into her pocketbook, having just called Jerome to let him know that she had arrived. *Spending the contract money already I see,* she mused, looking at the SUV as she exited her convertible and walked briskly up to Jerome's front door. She opened it and went inside.

She gasped and leaned against the door for support. Her knees felt like jelly. Jerome was lying on the couch. He was naked. He was hard. His dick was pointing skyward, veins prominent and bulging. It looked like it was upset with someone. Whoever had said that the penis did not have muscles had clearly never laid eyes on Jerome's shaft. She removed her shades and feasted her eyes for a few moments longer. Jerome looked like something from out of a wet dream. She slipped off her summer dress and stepped out of her sandals, leaving them at the door.

Jerome watched as she approached, admiring her well preserved body. A landing strip now decorated her pussy. There was nothing there the last time he saw her naked. He pussy glistened in the sunlight beaming in through the open windows. She was soaked.

Purring like a hungry cat, she slid to her knees and held his dick lovingly, rubbing her face all over it.

"God I missed your dick...this beautiful monster... it's the eighth wonder of the world."

Jerome moaned as she drooled on it and stroked it with both hands.

"Mmmm...this is just what the doctor ordered... oh yeah," she murmured, licking him languidly from his scrotum to his glans and back again. She then took him inside her mouth. She concentrated on the bulbous head first, licking the slit, then pursing her lips and sucking it. She then took him in halfway, slurping noisily as she sucked him with gusto, looking up at him occasionally, her blue eyes sparkling with lust and desire.

Jerome groaned and ran his hand through her short hair. She had cut it since he last saw her. It suited her. Played a role in helping her look much younger than her forty-five years.

Jerome moaned like a wounded animal as Elizabeth held his legs back and licked him from his scrotum to his anus. Jerome squirmed and grunted with his eyes tightly clenched as she tossed his salad. The pleasure was damn near unbearable. He couldn't take it anymore. He stopped her and retrieved a condom which he quickly rolled on.

"Let me ride you Jerome...I want to feel you in my throat..." she whispered hoarsely as she pushed him down onto the couch and climbed on top of him.

She reached for his mammoth shaft and held it at the entrance of her dripping orifice. She slid downwards gently until he was buried to the hilt. Beads of perspiration broke out on her upper lip and she gritted her teeth, breathing loudly as she gyrated on his hardness, milking it, squeezing it, relishing it. She could feel her first orgasm building up steadily. She increased her tempo, going up high and slamming down hard, her incredibly wet pussy making strange noises, as she rode hard and fast towards the promised land of orgasmic rapture.

"Oh God! I missed this dick so much! Nothing compares! Ohhhhh! I'm coming! I'm coming you big dick bastard! I'm coming you handsome brute! Fuck! Fuck! Fucccck!"

Elizabeth squeezed her nipples as she climaxed. She shook like a rag doll, her pussy secreting fluids at an alarming rate. Her orgasm went on and on, and when it finally subsided, she slumped on Jerome's broad chest, temporarily spent, whimpering with pleasure as her body spasmed intermittently, reeling from the intensity of her gut-wrenching climax.

Detective Corporal Spence walked away from the riveting scene. He had been watching through the open window and by God, what a show. He wanted to watch some more but was getting too turned on. His hands shook as he lit a cigarette and climbed into his Toyota Corolla. Wow. Watching the rich upper class woman behaving like a carnal animal had rattled him. He had watched his fair share of porn in his forty-two years but none compared to what he had just witnessed.

His suspicions were confirmed. Elizabeth Rhoden had a hand in killing her husband. There was no way that she could be truly grieving and be in there getting the stuffing fucked out of her. But his superiors would not view this as evidence. Strange, perhaps, but certainly not against the law. And he would get in trouble for unauthorized surveillance. But at least he had satisfied himself. He now undoubtedly knew the truth though there was nothing that he could do about it.

He whipped out his mobile to call Renita, his girl-friend. If she was home he'd swing by for a quickie. Watching Elizabeth Rhoden in action had given him an erection that refused to go down.

CHAPTER 16

After his torrid session with Elizabeth Rhoden, Jerome showered, changed and went to meet Gunner at the restaurant and bar where he and Lola were chilling.

"Damn...you bought all the clothes that Kingston has to offer," Jerome commented when he saw all of the shopping bags at their feet.

Lola smiled and sipped her white wine.

"Have a drink with us and then we can go to meet Angela. What time does she finish working?" Gunner said, beckoning to the bartender for an extra glass. Gunner then poured Jerome a drink from the small bottle of Hennessy that he had purchased along with some cranberry juice.

"Her last client was supposed to be at 3:30 so she should be home by now," Jerome replied. He sat down and took a sip. A group of three young girls came over giggling, and the shortest one, her voluptuous body stretching her black leggings to capacity, asked him to take a picture with them. Jerome obliged and took a group shot as well as solo shots with each of them. He also signed his autograph. The voluptuous one wanted hers on her panties much to everyone's amusement. Jerome told her that he wouldn't mind but the setting wasn't appropriate. She gladly gave him her mobile number to take a rain check.

Jerome watched her as she walked off, putting an extra twitch in her wide hips. Her ass was ridiculous. He definitely wouldn't mind spanking that.

Thirty minutes later, they made their way out to the parking lot. It was almost five p.m.

Time to head over to Angela's apartment.

Lenky frowned as he terminated the call. This was his fifth call to Eduardo, one of his Dominican customers based in Miami, over the last couple of days. His phone was off and though Lenky had left several messages, Eduardo had not called back. Very strange. Lenky hoped that he would hear from him soon. It was time to collect the balance of the payment for last month's shipment and this month's shipment would be ready to be sent to him next week.

He was at a warehouse off Hagley Park Road. The trailer with the marijuana from Westmoreland had arrived and he was ensuring that all was well. He lit his marijuana joint and listened to the light banter of the three cops that had escorted it safely into

Kingston. They were in a jovial mood. Lenky didn't blame them. They would be well paid.

Khianna called Laura just as she was about to leave the hairdresser. She was on the road and wanted to know if Laura wanted to hang out. Laura picked her up from the studio where her brother worked as an engineer. They stopped at Chang & Chung in Constant Spring and got some Chinese take-out. They then headed to Laura's home.

Laura dumped the food on the kitchen counter and instructed Sophia, the helper, to serve them by the pool. Scorcher, the new chef, was cooking dinner. He was making dumplings, mashed potatoes, boiled green bananas and country style stewed chicken. Laura had complained that he was cooking too much rice so he had decided to only cook rice on Sundays. He glanced at the food Laura had brought home as the helper prepared to serve it. He noticed without comment that there was rice. It was shrimp fried rice but it was still rice. He shook his head and tasted the gravy for the chicken.

It needed more pepper.

"Honey?" Jerome called out as he used his key to get inside Angela's apartment. She had given him a set of keys two weeks ago. He had not returned the gesture and she didn't seem to expect him to. Gunner and Lola trooped in behind him, laughing about something Lola had shared with him.

"I'm upstairs baby, give me a sec," Angela called down.

Jerome told Lola and Gunner to make themselves at home and he went into the kitchen to retrieve a cutting board and his stash of marijuana that he kept inside one of Angela's cupboards.

Angela came downstairs after a few minutes.

She bent down and gave Jerome a quick kiss.

"Baby, this is my best friend Gunner and his girl-friend Lola," Jerome said. "This is Angela, my future wife."

Angela blushed and Gunner got up and gave her a hug.

"Nice to meet you, I've heard so much about you," he said.

"All nice and wonderful things I hope," she teased.

"Most definitely, and it appears to be all true," Gunner responded.

"Oh Lord...two charmers...we can't allow them out of our sight Lola," she joked, as she gave Lola a hug.

Lola chuckled.

"I totally agree Angela...we're going to have to keep them under lock and key."

The men grinned, pleased to see that the two women liked each other right off the bat.

Angela went and got some drinks, assisted by Lola, and the foursome watched a comedy on DVD. They all indulged in the marijuana. The weed was potent, and it magnified the jokes on screen tenfold, making the four of them laugh hysterically at even the smallest joke.

The evening was off to a fun start.

"Mmmm...that hit the spot," Laura commented as she wiped her lips with a napkin. She had polished off a healthy serving of sweet and sour chicken and shrimp fried rice. "Some white wine would really put the icing on the cake."

Khianna smiled in mock sympathy.

"Awww hush...I'll have some for the both of us."

She then went inside to get a chilled bottle of wine and a glass.

Laura sighed. She couldn't wait to get rid of this baby. She couldn't even have a drink for Christ's sake. She really hoped that Jerome came through for her soon.

Khianna returned and poured herself a glass of the Chardonnay.

"Bitch," Laura said, watching her enviously.

Khianna cackled.

"But I'm a bitch with a drink," she responded, taking a sip and sighing with exaggerated pleasure.

Laura rolled her eyes. She leaned back in the chair. She squirmed restlessly. Wanting a drink wasn't her only problem. She was extremely horny. Her clit was throbbing painfully. Seeing and kissing Jerome had set her fireplace ablaze. She *needed* a release. She was so horny that she would've welcomed even Lenky between her legs. He could at least eat her out until she climaxed.

Laura sighed heavily.

"What's wrong L...you want a drink that bad?" Khianna asked, as she finished off her first glass and refilled it.

"Yeah...but I'm so fucking horny too. My clit feels like a dick. It's so damn hard."

A strange expression came over Khianna's face. She sipped her wine and looked at Laura steadily.

"Would you like me to take care of it for you?"

Laura was stunned. She wasn't into women but somehow Khianna's offer did not repulse her. Could she really allow a woman to make love to her? Her pussy throbbed an emphatic yes.

"I didn't know that you were into women," Laura responded, trying to keep her cool. Inwardly she was a turbulent sea of surprise, confusion and excitement. Surprised that she was actually open to the idea, confused as to why she would be, and excited by the notion of Khianna touching her intimately.

"Yeah...on and off for the last seven years," Khianna told her. "I was seduced by an older woman when I was seventeen and I liked it. But you know how homophobic most Jamaicans are so it's nothing that I broadcast."

Laura knew only too well, thinking back to Bigga's murder last month because he was found out to be a homosexual.

Laura looked at Khianna's tongue ring as she spoke. "Let's go inside..." she said throatily.

"This is absolutely delicious, Sara," Dr. Muirhead said, as he chewed slowly, savouring the taste of the sumptuous lamb. Sara had offered to cook dinner for him at his apartment. He had been skeptical that she had any culinary skills, as he knew that she grew up in a very privileged home and most likely did not have to cook. But she had surprised him. The lamb was superb and went perfectly with the white rice and garden salad.

"Thank you darling," Sara replied, smiling. She was pleased that he was enjoying the meal. She hadn't cooked in awhile and was a bit nervous but it had turned out well.

"Where did you learn to cook like this sweetheart?" he asked, really tucking into the food now.

"I used to watch my mother and the helper... picked up on a few things. Then when I lived on my own I found that I liked to cook and wasn't too bad at it."

"You're a very good cook...I'm going to put on a lot of weight messing with you," Dr. Muirhead said, smiling tenderly. He really, really loved this girl. He was still amazed that she wanted him. It had taken him many sleepless nights to truly believe that her affection was from the heart and not as a result of a compulsion to show him gratitude for helping her to conquer her demons.

She had done wonders for his ego and self-esteem, both of which had taken a beating from his wife Renita. The biggest blow had been coming home and seeing his wife of seven years on her hands and knees, screaming for the man behind her, who happened to be pounding her while holding a gun to the back of her head, to fuck her brains out. After seven years of marriage that was how he came to know that his wife was into kinky sex. She had shown no remorse at being caught, and the smirking cop had finished the deed before leaving in his own good time.

He had never been so ashamed, emasculated, embarrassed and angry in his life. He had killed them both a million different ways in his mind, but in reality, he was a gentle soul, couldn't hurt a fly. He had filed for divorce immediately. Something he should have done many years ago. She had never loved him. And when she realized that he didn't make as much as she thought he did, she made their marriage a living hell.

What the fuck you mean we can't afford a Mercedes? This is a fucking joke. You're not a real doctor. You're a broke ass quack.

That had been at the beginning, the first year. And when his practice grew, and he could afford one, by then he was smart enough not to let her know. She didn't even know about this apartment. He had gotten it at a good price from a colleague who had migrated to Canada two years ago. Thank God that had happened, as he now had a place to live.

At least they didn't have any children, which was great for more than one reason. Any spawn of Renita was bound to be evil and children being in the picture would have made it difficult for him to leave the marriage no matter how terrible it was. He hoped that the divorce became final soon. He couldn't understand why she was fighting it. She didn't love him and she would get the house. What more could she possibly want?

"A well fed man is a contented man," Sara told him, breaking into his reverie.

Dr. Muirhead couldn't argue with that.

"Angie, are you coming down to Montego Bay as well?" Lola asked, looking over at Angela. The two couples were snuggled up on either side of the living room, watching music videos. The comedy was over and they were all high and more than a bit tipsy, having polished off an ounce of marijuana and a bottle and a half of champagne.

Lola hoped that she would. She thought Angela was so sweet and classy, yet down to earth. It would be nice having her with them at Reggae Sumfest.

"Yeah but not until Friday night...I'll be flying down. The rest of the week is going to be pretty hectic," Angela replied, her voice low and husky. She couldn't believe how natural it had felt smoking marijuana in front of two people that she just met. She didn't have a problem indulging every now and then in private but would never in a million years think that she would have been comfortable to do it in front of others.

"Ok that's not so bad...you'll only miss dancehall night," Lola said, absently caressing Gunner's prominent cheekbones.

The world renowned reggae festival kicked off with a beach party on Wednesday, followed by dancehall night on Thursday and international nights one and two on Friday and Saturday respectively. Erykah Badu, one of Angela's favourite artistes, would be performing on Friday night. She couldn't wait to see her in action.

"Yeah...as long as I don't miss Erykah Badu I'm good," Angela told her.

"I'm looking forward to seeing Alicia Keyes on Saturday night," Lola said.

"You kind of resemble her baby...but you're prettier," Gunner chimed in. Lola chuckled happily and kissed him.

"I love you," she told him and they gazed at each other like there was no one else in the room.

"Ummm...there's a guest room upstairs...the one on the left," Angela told them, grinning.

Gunner smiled and got up in response. He lifted Lola like she weighed only twenty pounds and carried her upstairs.

Jerome and Angela watched them smiling. The house was full of love. And lust.

"They make such a nice couple," Angela commented, sighing as Jerome nibbled her ear.

"Yeah...almost as nice as us," Jerome agreed, moving his lips down to her neck.

"Mmmm...oh baby...shouldn't we go upstairs," Angela moaned as Jerome sucked on her neck gently and massaged her breasts through her baby T. Her nipples were as hard as ackee seeds. "Mmmmm... baby...suppose they come back downstairs...mmmm ...that would be embarrassing..."

Jerome snaked a hand between her legs and cupped her quivering mound through her shorts as he pulled his dick out through his fly.

"Shut up and suck your dick," he told her, his eyes glazed with want.

Angela's pussy pulsed at his words. Her man was high and in a rough mood. That's the vibe she was on too. She didn't feel like making love. She wanted to fuck. She had a feeling that tonight was going to be even crazier than usual.

She lowered her head and took his throbbing shaft into her mouth. Damn right it was her dick.

Jerome gripped her hair and groaned appreciatively.

He heard loud, rapid fire Spanish coming from upstairs. Lola was a screamer. Another thing she and her new found friend Angela had in common.

Angela would join her soon enough.

He closed his eyes and relished the feel of her hot, knowledgeable mouth.

He felt like he was levitating above the sofa.

Laura savoured her first kiss by a woman. It was different. Had the same qualities as being kissed by a man: soft, gentle, sweet, passionate, sensuous and probing; yet it was different. Just felt different. Khianna had large, pouty lips, and they felt really nice locked against hers. Her wine-coated tongue searched her mouth for forbidden pleasures, creating ripples in her body along the way.

Khianna broke the kiss, tugging gently on Laura's bottom lip. She smiled and kissed her way down to Laura's large breasts, massaging and caressing them with her tongue.

"Mmmm...your breasts are magnificent L...so big and firm...and juicy..."

Laura gasped as Khianna sucked and licked her left nipple. She looked up at the ceiling, trying to remember to breathe as Khianna made exquisite love to her, abandoning her breasts to head down south, her full lips and tongue wreaking havoc every where they touched. Laura's body was on fire. She clutched the sheets as Khianna licked and kissed the inside of her thighs, inching tantalizingly close to her anxiously awaiting pussy before moving away.

It was sweet torture. Laura's clit throbbed painfully. Her pussy was shedding erotic tears. Her thighs were moist with her juices and Khianna's wet kisses. She could feel Khianna's breath on her clit. She swore that it was going to burst. Khianna licked it. Laura's heart skipped a beat. She was clutching the sheets so tightly that her knuckles hurt. Khianna licked her pussy languidly, flicking her tongue ring against Laura's clit.

Laura's orgasm was sudden and powerful. Different from any that she had ever experienced. Her pupils dilated. Her mouth was wide open but no sound was forthcoming. Her body was as stiff as a corpse. It was like an out of body experience. She might have passed out for a few seconds, she wasn't sure. She felt disoriented, lost in a haze of pleasure.

Khianna's tongue was probing inside her pussy now, moving around with familiarity, like it had been there many times before. Laura started twitching and squirming, completely revived and ready for another excursion to ecstasy. There was no substitute for a good dick, especially Jerome's, but this was a close second.

Having a woman make love to her was an amazing experience.

As her breathing became shallow, and her pussy vibrated, announcing the arrival of her second orgasm, she wondered if she would try it again.

Her body shuddered and she held Khianna's head in place, flooding her mouth with her juices as she groaned and writhed in primal ecstasy.

She knew there was no doubt that she would.

CHAPTER 17

Jerome felt reinvigorated as he exited the pool and reached for his towel. He felt eyes on him as he dried his ripped, lean body. He glanced over to the apartment at the end of Angela's block and a middle-aged woman quickly moved away from the window. He had just done ten laps and was feeling pretty good, the effects of last night's debauchery slowing wearing off. He was hungry, and wondered if Angela had made breakfast before she left for work. Gunner and Lola were still in the guest room, lost to the world.

He made his way down the short block to Angela's apartment, nodding a greeting at the attractive, professionally attired young woman who was trying, and failing, not to stare at him. She smiled tightly, and hopped into her Mitsubishi SUV.

Jerome went inside and headed straight to the kitchen. Angela had indeed made breakfast. His protein shake, a concoction of eggs, milk and oats was in a container in the fridge, and there were scrambled eggs and bacon on the stove.

Jerome fixed himself a plate and sat at the kitchen counter. He turned on the small flat screen T.V. on the wall and watched sports highlights on ESPN. He checked the time. It was 9:45. If Lola and Gunner didn't get up by midday, he would wake them. They were supposed to be meeting up with Lenky at the gas station in Dunrobin at 2 p.m. so that they could all head out to Montego Bay for Reggae Sumfest.

Jerome was looking forward to the trip despite the tension between Gunner and Lenky. He was sure that they would have a ball in the second city nonetheless.

His mind ran on Laura and his promise to help her abort the baby soon. He polished off the rest of his eggs and drank the last of his protein shake. He would deal with it when he got back to Kingston.

"What's up Lenky," Jerome said, giving Lenky a manly hug. Lenky was leaning against his Lincoln Navigator in the parking lot of the gas station and concessionary store sipping what appeared to be Hennessy and cranberry.

His entourage, who would be traveling in the Lexus RX 350 along with Lenky's Navigator, consisted of Blacka, Ping Pong, the three girls he had taken to the club the other night and Mission, an aspiring musician with a buzz on the streets and who was one of the opening acts on dancehall night.

"You start drinking already and you know you can't hold your liquor," Jerome teased.

Lenky laughed and told him an expletive good naturedly.

"So who else rolling with you?" Lenky queried, looking over at the Mercedes SUV and the BMW X5. The vehicles were tinted and no one, except for Jerome, had alighted.

"Gunner and his girl...and a few of Gunner's mates," Jerome told him nonchalantly. Gunner had decided to bring Bishop and his crew along for the ride.

Lenky frowned but didn't comment. After two of the girls from Lenky's entourage returned from the restroom, the four luxury vehicles, with their hazardous lights flashing, indicating that they were traveling together, headed out with Blacka leading the way in the Lexus RX350.

"Hey Angie!" Jean said, surprised and happy at the afternoon call from her best friend. "Good to hear from you busy bee."

Angela smiled guiltily as she ate a spoonful of her yogurt.

"I know...I know...I've been neglecting you but it's your fault."

"My fault!" Jean exclaimed.

"Yep...in case you've forgotten, you're the one who hooked me up with a fellow named Jerome James... and he takes up a lot of my time," Angela said, making poor Jerome the scapegoat.

Jean laughed. "Well I guess that's a good excuse."

"Not to worry, let's have movie night tonight, you choose," Angela told her. "Jerome is on his way to Montego Bay so perfect time for us to catch up."

"Well thank God for Reggae Sumfest," Jean commented dryly.

Angela chuckled. "Don't be like that my honey... you know you're my best friend in the whole wide world no matter what."

"Whatever, you're paying tonight, for the movies *and* dinner."

Angela agreed readily and told her that she would pick her up at 7 p.m. That would give them enough time to have dinner and catch the 8:30 movie. She smiled as she put the phone down. Jean could be very needy at times but she was the best friend that a girl could ask for. Angela checked the time. It was 3 p.m. Time for Mrs. Boorasingh, an Indian woman with a bad back and a sour disposition.

She went inside the bathroom to quickly wash up.

The four vehicles pulled up at Faith's Pen, a popular food spot at the bottom of Mount Rosser. There were several tourists there as well as some locals, who seemed to be on their way to Montego Bay as well.

Everyone alighted from the vehicles and after ignoring the rush from the owners of the various food stalls who were trying to get the group to purchase from them, everyone followed Jerome over to the stall that he chose.

The cook grinned broadly that the football star had chosen to purchase from him. With such a large group he would make a tidy sum, enough to make up for the slow morning he'd had unlike some of his more vocal peers. Sometimes hanging back and letting the customers choose without being in their faces paid off.

The group ordered steam fish, calalloo, fried dumplings, festival, roasted corn, jerk chicken, fried fish and jerk pork. They sat in the vehicles and on the concrete benches and ate, listening to music. Mission, Lenky's friend who would be performing at the festival as an opening act, entertained them by performing a couple of his songs accapella.

Half an hour later they resumed their journey without incident, though Jerome had noticed that Lenky frowned when he saw Gunner's friends. He had recognized Bishop, and wondered aloud to Jerome why Gunner felt it necessary to be traveling with one of Jamaica's most wanted men.

"They are good friends," Jerome had offered, biting into his jerk pork.

"Seems like he's scared of something or someone," Lenky had said, chuckling derisively. "But if something is supposed to happen to him, not even God, much less Bishop, can help him," he added matter-of-factly.

Jerome had not responded.

He did not mention Lenky's words to Gunner. He didn't want to inflame the situation.

He shook his head as they went through Fern Gully. All he wanted was for everyone to have a good time. All this tension was so stupid and unnecessary.

Why couldn't everyone just get along?

CHAPTER 18

L aura got out of the shower and slipped on a T-shirt after moisturizing her sexy frame. She sighed longingly. With Lenky gone for four days it would have been the perfect opportunity to spend some time with Jerome and get some much needed TLC. But Jerome was in Montego Bay as well. She went downstairs to the kitchen to get some juice. Khianna was coming by to spend the night. She was going to bring some toys. Should be interesting. Last night was incredible. Khianna had given her three earth shattering orgasms. She wondered what tricks she had up her sleeve tonight.

Her pussy was wondering too.

It pulsed as she sipped her mango juice.

"Hi baby," Angela said, smiling as she answered the call. She was at Jupiter, a seafood restaurant that she hadn't been to in awhile. It was under new management and they had recently remodeled the place so she decided to take Jean there for dinner. It was a good decision. The food and the ambience were vastly improved.

"Hey honey bun," Jerome said, holding the phone to his ear with his shoulder as he rolled a marijuana joint. "Just wanted to let you know that we reached down safely. I'm at the villa now relaxing."

"Ok baby, I'm having dinner with Jean and then we're going to see a movie."

"Ok cool. Tell her hi for me. I love you baby. Catch you later."

"Love you too boo...kisses."

Angela slipped the phone into her pocketbook and took a sip of her red wine.

"Jerome said to tell you hi."

Jean grinned. "Cool. I'm so glad you guys hooked up. It's obvious he makes you very happy. Your face looks like a billboard out in Las Vegas whenever you say his name."

Angela blushed. "How would you know...you've never been to Vegas."

"Whatever, I have cable. I think I should change my name to cupid."

Angela rolled her eyes and took a bite of her dinner roll. She was forever in Jean's debt though. If Jean hadn't given Jerome her number...she shuddered at the thought. He was so much a part of her that she could not remember what her life used to be like before he entered it. She loved him so much that if he didn't propose, she would. She chuckled inwardly at the thought. Her daddy would have a fit.

Jada was not in a good mood. She had wanted to go to Reggae Sumfest with Lenky but he told her no. She could go on her own with a few friends but she wouldn't be able to have access to where Lenky would be. Only celebrities, entertainers and the media were allowed in that section. She knew that he had not taken his wife because she was pregnant so she couldn't understand why he didn't want to take her.

She had also called Karen several times for the day and she had not picked up or returned her calls. They had not spoken since the incident at Mikey's wake and she was missing her. Karen was really good company. She decided to walk over to Karen's house which was only five minutes away.

The five minute walk took her ten minutes as she stopped twice to converse with people that she knew. She called out to Karen as she opened the gate and went up to the verandah. The grill was locked but the front door was open. Karen came by the door after the fourth time that Jada called her name.

She leaned against the door jam and looked at Jada. She did not speak.

"Karen...why yuh behaving like that? So mi did wrong for leaving you up there but come on...I was angry. Keeping malice with me over that is fuckery."

Karen shook her head sadly.

"Go and ask Lenky's henchmen what they did to me...maybe then you'll understand the consequences of your actions," Karen told her softly, as she stepped inside and closed the door.

Jada was exasperated. Why the fuck was Karen shutting her out and talking in parables? Here she was, trying to make peace and Karen couldn't just chill the fuck out and let them move on from what was a simple incident in her estimation.

Jada sucked her teeth and exited the yard, slamming the gate. Fuck it. Their friendship was over. She was done trying. She wasn't even going to ask any of Lenky's men about what happened that night.

She didn't give a shit.

Jerome walked down to the beach, which was only a few meters away from the villa. They had rented the two, four bedroom villas on the exclusive beachfront property in Rosehall. The villas cost US$3500 per night and they had rented them for four days. Jerome had made the arrangements as he knew the owner of the property, a lawyer who was on the board of the Jamaica Football Association. Lenky had paid for one and Gunner had paid for the other.

He could hear Ping Pong talking loudly and excitedly about something while the others guffawed. He sipped from his plastic cup of Hennessy and cranberry and sat down on the sand, enjoying the feel of the cool water lapping at his bare feet. A shadow suddenly loomed over him, startling him a bit.

Jerome looked around. It was one of the girls that Lenky had brought with him. The cutest and most voluptuous of the three. She was wearing a T-shirt over the bottom of a red bathing suit. It was obvious that she wasn't wearing a bra. Her breasts were perky and slightly more than a handful, the nipples at attention, saluting the cool sea breeze.

"Hi...mind if I join you?" she said, the smile playing at the corners of her juicy lips saying that there was no way on earth that he would mind.

He didn't. He gestured for her to sit. She did, very close to him. Jerome breathed in her scent. Her perfume was very nice. Feminine and subtle.

"Where are you from?" Jerome asked, having noticed that she had an accent.

"Originally from Trinidad but I've lived in New York since I was six," she responded.

"I see...how long ago was that?"

She laughed. "Is that your way of asking my age... don't worry I'm legal. I'm twenty-one years old."

She had an infectious laugh. Jerome chuckled.

"So...I'm Amelia. I already know who you are... I've had a crush on you for over two years. When I saw you at the club that night when I was hanging with Lenky I wanted to come over to you so bad...but

I didn't want Lenky to get upset. He paid for me and my best friends' tickets to come to Jamaica and chill for two weeks. The other light skinned girl is my best friend and the tall slim chick is from Jamaica. I met Lenky through her."

Jerome sipped his drink. Interesting. Amelia started to toy with the draw strings on his Ralph Lauren beach shorts.

"So you like rolling with gangsters huh?" Jerome asked.

"Not particularly, I like rolling with rich guys... Lenky is rich, he just happens to be a gangster. Jerome it's like this...I'm in my sophomore year at Howard University and I know what I want out of life. College life is supposed to be the best, most fun years of your life...that grace period before its time to face the real world and make your mark. So I'm simply having fun. Coming to Jamaica with my closest friends, hanging out in VIP everywhere we go, staying at a swanky hotel, eating at the finest restaurants, going to Reggae Sumfest...and it doesn't cost me anything? You can't beat that."

"I'm sure it cost you something..." Jerome commented wryly.

Amelia laughed and shrugged. "Yeah I have to fuck him and suck his dick but he isn't well endowed and he comes fast every time. No skin off my back really."

Jerome laughed and shook his head. This girl was something else. But he liked her. She didn't beat around the bush, just told it like it was with no apologies.

"So what are you doing out here now...aren't you afraid he'll get upset with you?"

A look of uncertainty came over her pretty face but she shrugged and smiled.

"I've been hoping to catch you alone...I've been wet since I saw you hop out of the SUV at the gas station. I couldn't let this opportunity pass...had to at least try...you have no idea how many times I've dreamt about fucking you."

Her fingers grazed his crotch, almost innocently, as she continued to play with the draw strings on his shorts. Jerome looked at her. There was something to be said about a beautiful woman who would risk an ass whipping to fulfill her fantasy. And risking one she was indeed. Lenky was a very possessive man when it came to chicks that he really liked. And he surely must like this one. She was as pretty and as stacked as Laura. The girl had a face and body that could only have been designed by a man. She had the entire package.

"Take it out," Jerome breathed.

He could see her eyes in the moonlight. They were brimming with lust and anticipation. She bit on her bottom lip sexily as she slowly pulled his shorts down a bit. She gasped audibly when his shaft sprang free. Her eyes went from his crotch to his face and back again.

"Sweet Jesus..." she murmured.

Jerome tilted his head back in ecstasy as she lowered her head and licked his genitals all over, her tongue tracing the protruding veins all the way to the top and back down to the base. Moaning, she then took as much as of him as she could in her mouth.

Jerome groaned loudly as he looked up at the stars, the cool breeze caressing his bare back as her hot mouth devoured him hungrily.

He didn't care if anyone saw them.

CHAPTER 19

Jerome stepped outside to join the others. They were all dressed and ready to go to the Reggae Sumfest beach party. It was now midnight and the venue was roughly a twenty minute drive from the villa.

Lola gasped and everyone followed her eyes. It was Amelia. She had a Coach duffel bag in her hand. Her right eye was black and blue and her lips were swollen. So was her left cheek.

Jerome went over to her. He didn't have to ask what had happened. He told the others that he would be back in a minute and took Amelia to his room.

"He called me into his room as soon as I went back to the villa," she said to Jerome, sitting on the chair that was by the window. "Started to beat me up, asking me if I took him for a fool...if I thought that he had brought me here to fuck other men. Called me a whore...fucked me...beat me up again, then threw me out and told me to find my way back to

Kingston, and get my shit from out of the hotel room when I got there."

"Damn..." Jerome muttered. He wasn't exactly surprised that Lenky wasn't pleased that she had fucked him but he hadn't expected Lenky to beat her up so badly and throw her out.

"Just stay here and we'll figure something out tomorrow," Jerome told her. "Get your face cleaned up and put some ice on the swelling. There's a medicine cabinet in the bathroom. See you later," Jerome told her, squeezing her shoulder affectionately. He was sorry for her. Lenky didn't have to do her so badly.

"Thanks Jerome...thank you."

Jerome smiled and left the room.

Lenky and his entourage were now standing in front of the villa. There was tension in the air. Jerome wondered if they would make it through the four days without an altercation. It wasn't just Lenky either. Blacka and Ping Pong were obviously edgy whenever they were around Bishop, who, on the other hand, was always his cool, laid back self who seemed to be not paying anyone any mind though his eyes missed nothing.

It was like they felt that they had something to prove being around such a notorious gangster. Jerome greeted Lenky and they all trooped out to the parking lot. No mention was made of Amelia. Jerome noted Amelia's best friend and the other girl walking on either side of Lenky, holding on to his arms. They didn't seem perturbed about what had happened to their friend. Or maybe they were just afraid.

Everyone piled into their respective rides and the four vehicles headed out.

"Thanks for a great night Angie...you're forgiven for neglecting me," Jean said jokingly as Angela pulled up outside her gate.

"Why thank you...you're so kind," Angela smirked.

They hugged and Jean went inside. Angela waited until Jean closed the grill to the verandah and was safely inside before driving off. It had been a good evening indeed. Dinner was delicious and the movie, a suspense drama, had been entertaining.

She yawned and turned the radio to the jazz station as she headed down Mona Road. She was tired. All that hardcore sex from Jerome over the past few days had really worn her out. Yet she smiled at the thought of heading down to Montego Bay and seeing him on Friday night. She couldn't wait to get some more of the no-holds-barred-fuck-me-like-there's-no-tomorrow sex that Jerome had been treating her to lately.

My baby has certainly transformed me into a certified freak.

Even when she got home and climbed into bed she was still smiling.

One of the reps for the organizers of the festival met Jerome at the entrance of the VIP parking area and gave him enough armbands for everyone. They parked and then headed over to the VIP section of the party. A large crowd was on hand and the party was in full swing. They sauntered in, Jerome and Lenky stopping every now and then to converse with people that they knew. They settled down inside one of the large white VIP tents and Gunner ordered some champagne, Hennessy, red bull and cranberry juice from one of the scantily clad waitresses. They were all wearing white swim suits.

Lenky placed his own order and sat down on a sofa to the right, with either girl next to him. His boys were loosely scattered behind him and their chests puffed importantly when the DJ gave a shout out to Lenky and the crew.

Jerome, who was sitting with Gunner and Lola on one of the smaller sofas, was given several shout outs as well. The waitress returned quickly with their liquor and placed it on the small table next to the sofa. She begged Jerome to take a picture with her and he graciously obliged.

Jerome and Gunner, after pouring drinks, relaxed on the sofa and people watched. The women were out in their numbers and the VIP area was filled with sexy gold diggers, strutting their stuff in front of the plethora of drug dealers, celebrities and entertainers. Lola got up when the DJ switched to hip hop and stood in front of Gunner. Gunner smiled as he watched her dance. She was a good dancer, and she lost herself in the music, dancing like no one was watching, which they were. A lot of people were staring at her.

One of the gold diggers, perhaps jealous of Lola, walked by and bumped her intentionally, causing Lola to spill her drink. Lola, having noticed the girl giving her dirty looks from the moment that she had walked in, threw the remainder of her drink on the girl. Security moved quickly, pulling the girl away as she shouted and cursed at Lola angrily. Lola refilled her drink nonchalantly and kept on dancing.

Gunner looked at Jerome and grinned. Lola was something else.

He knew without a doubt that he was madly in love with her.

They left the beach party at 4:30 a.m. On the way to the villa, Ping Pong, who was driving the Lexus RX350, was a bit too intoxicated and ran into the back of Lenky's Lincoln Navigator. The damage wasn't too bad but Lenky, who hated to see minor scratches on any of his vehicles, was extremely pissed and Ping Pong received two punches to the face for his indiscretion.

When they got back to the villa, Lola and Gunner went skinny dipping on the beach while Jerome went to his room where Amelia was in his bed sleeping.

Jerome switched on the bedside lamp. He pulled

the covers down a bit. She opened her eyes and caught him watching her.

"Hey handsome...how was the party?" she asked sleepily.

"It was good. How are you feeling?"

She sat up and leaned against the bed head. Her breasts were exposed. Jerome gazed at them. They were a perfect pair. Mouthwatering and firm, they were just begging to be touched.

"I took a couple painkillers and cleaned the eye and stuff...so I'm not feeling too bad," she replied. "Besides you're here now...and I'm soaking wet...I dreamt about you," she added, looking at him seductively with her good eye. The result was comical. They both cracked up.

Her face was still swollen and the eye looked terrible but having cleaned up, she looked a lot better than she had when she first came over. Jerome truly admired her spirit. She was different. He had never met anyone quite like her.

He reached under the sheet and she spread her legs. Soaked was an understatement. His finger almost drowned. He rose and undressed. He was as hard as granite. She watched with anticipation as he rolled on a condom and brushed the sheets aside. No foreplay was necessary. She threw her legs onto his broad shoulders and he entered her with a firm thrust.

"Ohhhh... fuck yeah...mmmm...I've been dreaming about this all night...fuck me Jerome...tear my pussy up..."

Jerome went deep and hard, round and round, milking her pussy for all it was worth, making her shudder and moan in ecstasy with each stroke.

Amelia had no regrets about what had happened to her. She would take a daily ass whipping if she could get sex like this afterwards. Jerome's dick was like a genie, granting her pussy every conceivable orgasmic wish.

By the time he placed her on her hands and knees, and stroked her from behind half an hour and three mind-boggling orgasms later, Amelia was sure that her pussy was as swollen as her face.

CHAPTER 20

"This is so good," Amelia said, thoroughly enjoying her tender strips of chicken breast coated with Jamaican coconut and served golden brown with creamy mustard dipping sauce. Jerome was having baked potato skins filled with bacon and melted cheese. They were dining at London Bridge, a traditional styled English pub and restaurant. The owner, a pudgy businessman from England who had fallen in love with Montego Bay and moved to Jamaica ten years ago, recognized Jerome and after chiding him good-naturedly for signing with the wrong team instead of his beloved Liverpool, took a picture with him to put on his wall of fame.

Jerome smiled at her. With the swelling down a bit, make-up and her oversized Prada shades, her bruises were adequately hidden. Amelia was really good company. If Angela wasn't coming down he would've let her stay with him until he went back to Kingston. Though Lola and Angela had hit it off, he doubted Lola would have snitched on him. She seemed like the kind of woman that minds her own business. At least he hoped so.

They had gotten up at 11 a.m., showered and made some calls. Fortunately for Amelia, there was a domestic flight to Kingston leaving at 2:30 and it wasn't full.

She would fly in to Kingston and try to move up her flight to the earliest possible date or buy a one way ticket to New Jersey, whichever worked out cheaper or quicker. If she didn't get to leave today she would just stay at the hotel tonight. Though Lenky had told her to get her stuff out of the hotel room, he couldn't stop her, the room was already paid for up to Sunday and he would still be in Montego Bay.

"You were everything I imagined you would be times two," Amelia told him, dabbing her lips with a napkin. "You're handsome, sexy, free-spirited, well-hung, fuck like you invented sex...and to top it off you're really a nice person. Your girlfriend is a very, very lucky woman."

Jerome smiled but did not respond. Half an hour later they headed out to the airport.

"How far is the airport?" Amelia asked.

"Not far...about a fifteen minute drive from here," Jerome responded.

"Ok...let me see if I can make you come before we get there," she said, smiling devilishly.

She unzipped his fly and extracted his dick.

Jerome moaned when he felt her hot mouth.

He honked the horn in celebration when he climaxed ten minutes later.

Amelia didn't spill a drop.

Lenky took a deep drag off of his marijuana joint. The weed was potent, causing him to cough harshly as he exhaled. He sat up and took a sip of bottled water. He was in the hammock outside the villa, enjoying the light breeze. The villa had a state of the art kitchen so Lenky had sent Ping Pong and the two girls to purchase stuff to cook. The food was being prepared and he could smell the spicy curry chicken. His stomach growled in anticipation.

Lenky wasn't in the best of moods. Though Eduardo, his Dominican customer in Miami, had finally returned his call and they had spent over fifteen minutes catching up on business, his spirit was unsettled. He didn't like the way that Jerome was acting. Before Gunner, it had always been him and Jerome hanging. He had always looked out for Jerome like a brother, given him access to anything that he wanted, helped him out in anyway that he could and now it was all about Gunner. All of a sudden he was secondary.

Jerome had no loyalty. He knew Lenky longer, had met Gunner through him, and despite knowing how much Lenky hated Gunner's guts, he had still sided with Gunner. Lenky shook his head in disgust. He was also pissed at Jerome for getting involved in the situation with that bitch Amelia. He wasn't mad that Jerome had fucked her, she was a sexy slut and if he had been in Jerome's shoes he would have fucked her too, but Jerome shouldn't have put her up after he had disciplined her and sent her home.

"Yo boss, the food ready. You eating outside?" Blacka queried from the doorway, interrupting his thoughts.

Lenky got up and made his way inside. Eating a plate full of curry chicken, dumplings the size of cartwheels and boiled green bananas in a hammock would be a tricky undertaking.

CHAPTER 21

"Hey baby," Jerome said when Angela came on the line. He had stopped by a restaurant to get some Chinese takeout for everyone at the villa after dropping Amelia off at the airport. He was now ten minutes away from the villa.

"Hi sugar, how was the beach party?" she asked, plopping down on the easy chair in the therapy room. She had just finished up with Mrs. Gibson, who had a back injury that she suspected was caused by her abusive husband, who was a Pastor of all things.

"It was good…we didn't get in until 5 this morning. How's work?"

"Ok cool, wish I could've been there. It's going ok. I miss you…"

"I miss you too baby…can't wait to see you on Friday."

"I dreamt about you last night. You were doing all sorts of naughty things to me," Angela said, laughing.

"You've turned your angel into a freak."

"Yeah," Jerome agreed, "fucked her wings off her back and broke her halo."

Angela laughed hysterically.

"I love you boy...very much."

"I love you more..."

They chatted until Jerome got to the villa. He parked, held the phone to his ear with his left shoulder, retrieved the three bags of food from the back seat, nudged the door shut, and headed over to the villa.

Gunner was on the patio with Lola.

"About bloody time mate...we're starving," he said, hopping up from off the lounge chair to help Jerome with the bags.

"Let me say hi to Lola," Angela said.

Jerome handed Lola the phone saying that her new best friend wanted to talk to her.

He headed inside and Gunner, Bishop and the rest of the crew were busy sharing the food, anxious to eat. He was still full from the lunch that he had with Amelia so he made himself a drink, Hennessy and cranberry.

A soccer game on the flat screen caught his attention. He scooped some weed up from off the weed board and sat in front of the TV and proceeded to roll himself a joint. It was a Champions League match between AC Milan and Arsenal. It was a dream of his to not only play in the Champions League, but to hoist the trophy as part of the winning team one day. It wasn't far fetched, Manchester FC, whom he had signed a contract with, was one of the three top clubs in England, and as such qualified for the Champions League every season, last winning it two years ago in a thrilling final against Barcelona. His fate was in his hands. Stay healthy, work hard and live up to his potential, and the rest would take care of itself.

Lola came inside still talking on the phone.

"Angie, I gotta go, see you tomorrow, I'm so hungry I can't see straight," Lola said and held out the phone to Jerome. He put the weed aside and took it.

"Yeah babe," Jerome said.

"Ok honey, gonna get back to work, my next appointment is in five minutes."

"Let me give you a laugh before you go...a woman turns to her husband in bed and asks him if he loved her only because her father died and left her a fortune. The husband replies, 'That's crazy, of course not. I'd love you no matter who left you the money.'"

"That's horrible!" Angela said, though she was laughing.

"I love you baby, catch you later."

"Love you too, bye."

The security at the front gate buzzed the villa to let

them know that the shuttle had arrived to pick them up. Jerome glanced at his watch. It was exactly 9 p.m. Right on time as Mr. Pendergrast, one of the festival organizers who owned the villa where they were staying and who was on the board of the Jamaica Football Association, had promised. Jerome was grateful for the VIP service. Driving there on one's own and trying to get good parking was a nightmare at a festival of this magnitude. The shuttle would take them directly to the back stage entrance and would be there to take them back home whenever they were ready.

Jerome called Lenky on his mobile to let him know that it was time to go. Lenky gruffly told him ok and hung up the phone. Jerome had walked over to visit Lenky earlier that evening but hadn't stayed long. Lenky was acting weird. Jerome realized that things would never be the same between him and Lenky. He was cool with that. He didn't have the time or patience to be dealing with petty nonsense. Gunner had treated him like a brother when he went to England to sign his contract. It was only right that he extended the same courtesy. Besides he genuinely liked the guy, he was really a brother from another mother. So if Lenky was upset because he had thought that he would've given Gunner the cold shoulder simply because he didn't like him, then so be it.

Sometimes things ran their natural course.

And perhaps their friendship had.

Lenky and his entourage sauntered out a few minutes later and they all made their way to the parking lot where the large air conditioned bus was waiting. Four people were already on the bus, a hardcore dancehall artiste who was scheduled to perform tonight and three people from her entourage. Obviously she had not yet put on the outfit that she would be performing in. She was dressed casually in jeans and a baby tee. Most of the artistes usually went all out with their outfits on dancehall night, as what everyone wore was usually a big topic of conversation in the streets in the days after the show, as much as the performances themselves.

Everyone got on board and the bus headed out on the 30 minute journey. The ride was mostly quiet, everyone more or less content to listen the music playing on the radio or the thoughts swirling in their heads.

The bus was stopped by security at the area by the backstage gate. A tall skinny security officer, along with a representative for the festival, came on board.

"Good night everyone," the representative said. The security guard remained silent.

The representative then dealt with the female entertainer and the people with her first, and they exited the bus after putting on their special wristbands. He then spoke with Jerome, whom he had been instructed to go to and then issued wristbands to everyone in his party.

"No one is armed right?" he said to Jerome, but loud enough for everyone to hear.

"Nah, it's all good," Jerome assured him though he knew for a fact that at least seven people among them were armed with handguns. The security guard had a dubious look on his face and was itching to search them as there was a strict no weapons policy for the festival but as the rep didn't didn't push it, neither did he. After all, the rep was in charge.

Everyone got up and exited the bus in single file. They walked to the gate which was manned by three security officers and another festival rep in a black t-shirt with the words Reggae Sumfest emblazoned across the chest with the logo underneath.

They flashed their armbands and were admitted.

The VIP area was set up like a village. There were small private tents for artistes who needed to change and do make-up or just simply relax away from prying eyes, there were several bars including a Hennessy lounge, two large food tents, both buffet styled, and a large media tent where most of the interviews were taking place. Jerome saw tons of people that he knew and he stopped and chatted with them as he, Gunner, Lola and Bishop and his boys made their way to the Hennessy lounge, staying close together.

He didn't know or cared where Lenky and his goons were. Once they had gotten inside the venue, Lenky had stopped to speak with someone and Jerome had continued on. The act on stage was doing well for himself in the early going. The crowd was cheering on his performance. Some of the people in the VIP area were standing close to the side of the stage, watching the energetic artiste prance up and down as he rode the rhythm like a seasoned performer.

Gunner ordered two bottles of Hennessy and several bottles of cranberry and they placed their drinks along with a bucket of ice and plastic cups on one of the circular metallic tables that was beside the Hennessy lounge. It was a good spot, they could see the stage from there and they were out of the way of the people bustling back and forth.

Jerome felt eyes on him and looked to his right.

It was Cheetah.

She said something to Rocky, her manager, then walked over to him.

CHAPTER 22

L aura was feeling miserable. She wished that she was in Montego Bay or that Jerome was in Kingston. She was missing him terribly. Going through withdrawl symptoms. It had been too long since she had spent some quality time with him, having him deep inside her, taking her to places that only he could.

Her sexual adventure with Khianna had been a welcome distraction but the novelty was wearing off. After two nights of experiencing everything in Khianna's sexual arsenal, she was now back to square one, being depressed over her pregnancy and not being able to see Jerome. She had sent home Khianna a couple of hours ago, told her that she wanted to be alone.

She was in the bedroom, looking at her naked form in the full length mirror. She was still amazed that she had Jerome's seed growing in her belly. If the circumstances were different she would be a very happy woman. Ecstatic to be giving Jerome his first child. But as it stood the stress was getting to her, and the morning sickness and overall nausea was getting worse. But it wasn't all bad. Admittedly, she was glowing. Her voluptuous body looked ripe and her naturally full breasts were even fuller.

She sighed. After the abortion she would go to New York for a couple of weeks. Check on the restaurant, do some shopping, hang out with a few old friends.

The change of scenery should do her good.

"Hi Jerome," Cheetah purred, as she gave him a tight hug. She pulled back slightly and looked him up and down, taking in his red and black outfit. He was rocking a black Armani V-neck t shirt underneath a fitted black Armani blazer and slacks. A skinny red Prada belt and black Prada loafers completed the look. "You look great."

"Thanks," Jerome responded. "This is my friend Gunner and his girlfriend Lola. This is Cheetah, a friend of mine."

"Hi," Cheetah said, adding after giving Lola a quick scan, "nice shoes, girl."

"Thanks, you're that singer right?" Lola asked.

Cheetah nodded and smiled.

"I love your music...you have a very unique flavour."

"Thanks, I'm pleased you like my music. I have

some really hot stuff coming up...I received some out of this world inspiration the other day," Cheetah said, glancing at Jerome with a cheeky smile. "And I'm performing tomorrow night."

"Ok great, looking forward to seeing that," Lola said.

"Well it was nice meeting you guys. Jerome I'll catch you later."

The three of them watched her as she walked off. Cheetah was rocking the hell out of her cat suit inspired outfit, looking every bit like an R&B diva on the rise. Jerome could feel something else on the rise.

There was no question that he would be fucking her tonight.

Lenky was not having a good time. He was thinking about Mikey. The annual trek to Monetego Bay had been one of Mikey's favourite outings. There was a void not having him this year, or ever again. The situation with Jerome and Gunner was also eating at him. He despised disloyalty. So much so that when Jerome had come by the villa earlier he could barely stomach to talk to him. Jerome had really disappointed him. He supposed that he should talk to Jerome about it but that wasn't his style. It would make him seem weak. So fuck it. It was what it was. He was itching to spill some of Gunner's blood though.

The cocky motherfucker needed to be taught a lesson. Coming into his territory and acting like he was the man.

No respect.

He was not going to let it slide.

Oh God! I feel it in my throat! Jerome! Oh Jerome! Fuck! I'm coming!

"Wow..." Lola said, looking at Gunner as he puffed on a cigarette. They had finished having sex a few minutes ago and were relaxing in bed. They could clearly hear Cheetah in Jerome's room having the time of her life. "I dunno baby...I'm a bit uncomfortable being so cool with Angela and knowing that Jerome is over there fucking someone else."

Gunner exhaled and looked at her.

"I understand...but don't sweat it. Never interfere in anyone's relationship. Jerome loves Angela to bits, and she loves him. Anything there is to find out, let her find out on her own. They are both your friends...don't get involved."

Lola processed that for a few moments. She supposed that he was right. The messenger usually ends up with the short end of the stick. And somehow becomes the enemy after all is said and done. She wondered if she would want Angela to tell her if the situation was reversed. No. She wouldn't.

"You're right babe," she agreed.

Ahhhh! Oh my God! I can't stop coming!

Listening to Cheetah was making Lola horny again. She slid downwards and licked the inside of Gunner's thighs and his scrotum until his dick started to respond.

Then she took him in her mouth.

"Oh my God..." Cheetah whispered, still face down and ass up in the same position that Jerome left her in when he finally climaxed and went inside the bathroom to dispose of the condom and to take a leak. "My pussy is on fire."

Jerome laughed and smacked her on the right ass cheek.

"I'm gonna get some juice, want anything?"

"Yeah...a new pussy," Cheetah responded cheekily.

Jerome laughed again. Cheetah was a regular comedian. They had left the stage show at six in the morning, though there were two acts left to go. Lola had arched her eyebrows when she saw Cheetah coming back to the villa with them but had not commented. Jerome, Gunner, Lola, and Bishop and the boys had been the only ones on the bus. They had no idea if Lenky was still at the show or had gone home already, neither had anyone cared.

Jerome pulled on his boxers and went out to the kitchen. He glanced out in the living room. Two of

Bishop's boys were knocked out on the sofas, the bad guys in the action movie on the screen watching them. He retrieved two bottles of cranberry juice from the refrigerator and headed back to the bedroom.

Cheetah was still in the same position.

CHAPTER 23

Friday was a blur. The day sped by quickly as all everyone did was sleep, eat and sleep some more. Cheetah had left at midday to go to rehearsal. Jerome finally got up for good at 5 p.m. He, Gunner and Lola went down to the beach to swim and chill for an hour, then showered and got dressed. Angela was coming in on a 6:30 domestic flight.

"You think we need your boys to come with us?" Jerome asked, as he stood by Gunner's room door. Lola was already dressed. She was standing by the dresser, Coach tote bag in hand, looking like a model.

"Yep, that's why they're here...you never know when that coward might try something stupid innit," Gunner replied matter-of-factly as he tied the laces on his white Gucci tennis shoes. "He's not even talking to you now. Who knows what's next."

Jerome nodded solemnly. He watched as Gunner slipped a Glock 17c handgun inside the waistband of his Yves Saint Laurent jeans. He couldn't believe that things had deteriorated this far. But Gunner was right. You just never knew with Lenky. Violent and irrational was not exactly a good combination.

They headed out to the parking lot and climbed into their vehicles.

"What's up babes?" Lenky asked, as he exhaled a cloud of marijuana smoke. He had just had a threesome with the two girls and was now relaxing in his bedroom alone, enjoying a smoke.

"Nothing," Laura responded, struggling to keep the annoyance out of her voice. This was Lenky's fourth call for the day, and she was not in the mood to be chit chatting on the phone. "About to go take a nap."

"Ok, just checking up on you...miss you and I wish you could've been here."

Yeah me too, with Jerome.

"Yeah, too bad. Catch you later babe, I'm feeling really tired," Laura told him.

"Alright baby, love you."

"Love you too, later," Laura said, terminating the call.

Lenky placed the phone on the bedside table and flicked the ash off his marijuana joint onto the ash tray.

He didn't like the way Laura had sounded all day. She was giving off a weird vibe. He surmised that her moodiness was because of the pregnancy. Some women were like that, especially in the early stages.

He was supposed to be going home on Sunday but had changed his mind and would go home tomorrow instead. Skip the final night of the festival. There wasn't really anyone performing that night that he wanted to see. He missed his wife, and plus he had Calvin's wedding to attend on Sunday afternoon.

Yeah, he would go home tomorrow. He would swing by one of the luxury stores in Montego Bay and get Laura a new bag. A nice Louis Vuitton or something. She had a lot but a woman can never have too many bags or shoes, according to Laura. Also maybe a piece of jewellery.

That should help to cheer her up.

Angela's face lit up when she saw Jerome, Gunner and Lola standing by the SUV waiting for her. Jerome saw her and his face mirrored hers as he rushed over and scooped her up in his arms.

"Hey baby," he cooed, grinning, unconcerned about the many eyes on them.

She gave him a quick peck on the lips and he took her carry-on and placed it in the trunk.

She greeted both Gunner and Lola with hugs and they piled into the vehicle and headed out.

"Hungry baby?" Jerome asked.

"Starving," Angela responded. She hadn't eaten since a light lunch around 12:30.

Jerome headed over to Pork on the Pier, Montego Bay's premier spot for jerk pork. It was an expensive but popular chill spot, as the food was excellent and they provided live entertainment.

Angela noticed the black BMW X5 that had been behind them since they left the airport.

"I think that vehicle is following us baby," she said to Jerome.

"They are detective...brilliant job! They're with us babe," Jerome told her, pretending to wince as she punched him on the shoulder playfully for his sarcasm.

"Keep that up and you won't be getting any tonight young man," Angela teased.

"If you won't give it to me I'll take it..."

Angela's eyes glazed over.

"Stop it...before you have to pull over..."

"Hey, there are kids back here," Lola protested, prompting everyone to erupt in laughter.

This is what it should be all about, Jerome mused, as he pulled into the parking lot of the restaurant. *Good times with the people you love.*

CHAPTER 24

"Baby...do we have time for a quickie?" Angela asked in her most seductive voice as they undressed and climbed into the massive shower. Jerome turned on the hot water as she hugged him from behind. "Hmmm?"

Jerome closed his eyes as her hands moved down to his genitals.

She gave him tiny, sharp bites all over his back as she stroked him.

Groaning, Jerome turned around and lifted her up, holding her in the air against him with one hand as he used the other to place his hard member at the entrance of her already wet orifice. He rubbed it against her pussy for a few moments before sliding it in. Holding her with both hands now, Jerome stood directly underneath the shower head as he brought her up and down slowly, her sugar walls loving his dick with sweet wet kisses.

He was fucking her so slowly, so smoothly, that she could feel every bulging vein, every sweet inch, as he lovingly juiced her pussy like a ripe peach.

"Ohhhh...sweet Jesus...I missed you...only two days away and I missed you so much...I'm so in love with you baby..." Angela whispered; her breathing shallow as his one eyed monster displayed its perfect vision, finding her pleasure points effortlessly, already coaxing an orgasm to the surface.

Angela hugged him tightly; her hands and legs wrapped around him in a death grip, her contracting, gushing pussy squeezing his shaft in erotic gratitude, as she shook violently like an out of control vibrator.

Jerome followed immediately.

He grunted and had to summon all of his strength to stay on his feet as he climaxed deep inside her soul.

"I love her voice," Angela commented, listening in rapture as Cheetah, stylishly attired in black and white leggings, killer Jimmy Choos, and a black tuxedo-style jacket, introduced the massive crowd to *Pleasurable Pain*, her new unreleased track. "Very distinct and sultry."

"Yeah," Jerome agreed, quite pleased that he was the inspiration for such a hot song. "She's going to go far...she has the entire package."

Angela turned her head slightly to look at him. They were in a sky box close to the stage, a spot so exclusive that Jerome was only allowed to bring three people with him, so Angela, Lola and Gunner were up there with him while Bishop and the rest of the crew were in another VIP section down at the front of the stage. They would meet up down there when it was time to leave.

"This might be my new favourite song baby…that's exactly how you make me feel sexually."

Jerome smiled and kissed her cheek.

Lola, who was right beside them sipping a glass of champagne, could hear their conversation. She was sure that Angela's opinion of the song and the singer would drastically change if she found out that Jerome had made Cheetah hit higher notes than the ones that she was currently belting out on stage less than 24 hours ago.

Cheetah left the stage to thunderous applause and was called back for an encore.

Laura felt like she was going crazy. She had been seriously depressed for two days and was not getting any sleep. It was now 1 a.m. and despite barely getting a wink last night, sleep was nowhere in sight. Frustrated, she flung the covers aside and climbed out of bed. She noticed the red light on her mobile phone blinking and took it up from off the bed side table. She checked it as she went downstairs. It was a text message from Steel, the guy that she slept with whenever she spent time in New York. He was in Jamaica for Reggae Sumfest and was going to be in Kingston tomorrow to take care of some business. He wanted to know if she could see him as he wouldn't be going back to Montego Bay until Sunday morning.

Laura smiled for the first time in two days. Hell yeah, she could see him. Lenky wouldn't be back until Sunday so as soon as Steel finished up his business, she could be all his. She responded to his text, telling him that yes he could see her and that he should call as soon as he had finished conducting his business.

Jerome aside, who was in a class all by himself, Steel was the best lover that she had ever had. With Jerome unavailable, Steel was the next best thing. And he couldn't have materialized at a better time. Surely some good sex would go a long way in helping her to feel much better. So would a drink.

She hadn't been drinking because she was pregnant but what kind of sense did that make when she was going to have an abortion soon? Why should she deny herself? No more, she was going to have several drinks tonight.

It would help her insomnia.

She retrieved a bottle of champagne from the fridge, opened it, got a glass, and went upstairs.

CHAPTER 25

"That will be $160,000, sir," the pretty Indian clerk said to Lenky, looking at him with a bright smile.

Lenky was at a jewellery store at the Green Bay shopping center, an upscale mall located on the outskirts of Montego Bay. He had purchased a cute bracelet for Laura to go along with the Louis Vuitton clutch that he had purchased at A Taste of Europe, a luxury European goods store located on the same mall.

Lenky gestured to Blacka who handed him a black attaché case. Lenky opened it and counted out the cash from the neatly organized stacks of money.

"Oh, I thought you were going to pay by card," the clerk said, seemingly uncomfortable with such a large cash transaction.

"What, you don't take cash?" Lenky asked, smirking at her.

"Of course we do sir," she replied, smiling indulgently.

They completed the transaction and left the store. Lenky was pleased with his purchases. The gifts plus his early unexpected return should put a smile on his wife's pretty face.

Lenky checked the time. It was 11:16 a.m. If they made good time he would be in Kingston by the latest 2 p.m. He would then drop the girls off at the hotel and head straight home.

Steel's business associate dropped him off at Laura's at 12 p.m. Laura met him outside and quickly whisked him to the guest room upstairs, away from the prying eyes of the chef who was in the kitchen preparing lunch. She had sent home the helper at 11:30, telling her to take the rest of the day off.

"Look at you...as sexy as ever," Steel drawled, licking his lips as he took in her curves appreciatively. "You look great L...you're thicker than the last time I saw you...I like it."

Laura smiled and strutted sexily over to the love seat by the window. She was wearing a short dress, with no panties on. She sat with her legs slightly open, giving Steel a peek of her shaven mound.

"Thanks hun...I've missed you...when I saw your text I was elated. Lenky is out of town until tomorrow so you can spend the night," she told him, her pretty face sporting a devilish smile.

"Music to my ears," Steel grinned.

He unbuttoned his flannel shirt and tossed it onto the bed. His Timberland boots, cargo pants and boxer briefs followed. He padded over to her dressed only in his socks and the large rose gold chain that was so long that the medallion was almost touching the tip of his rock hard dick.

He knelt in front of her and pulled her dress up around her waist. He then placed her legs on his shoulders. He looked up at her. Laura bit her lips, her pussy jumping at the desire that she saw in his eyes. She emitted a soft moan.

"I'm gonna feast on this pussy until my jaws hurt," he promised. He then lowered his head.

Laura groaned at the feel of his large lips on her quivering mound. She badly wanted some dick but Steel was really good at oral. She'd let him make her come twice but that would be it.

Then he would have to fuck her into oblivion.

She needed to be properly fucked like she needed air.

Angela and Lola decided that they didn't want to eat out but would rather make use of the kitchen and cook dinner for their men. They had all gotten up at 11 a.m. and after a quick lunch went jet-skiing. When they got back to the villa Jerome and Gunner were given a grocery list and sent to the supermarket.

They were now watching a soccer match on TV along with Bishop and his crew, while the women worked their magic in the kitchen. The guys were starving, especially after smoking weed, but they were not allowed to eat anything until dinner was served as the women didn't want them to spoil their appetites.

Jerome's stomach grumbled in protest for what must be the twentieth time. Angela came out to the living room. She kissed him on the cheek for being a good sport and told them that the food would be ready in twenty minutes and that they would be happy they waited.

The food smelled good indeed but Jerome wondered if they would be alive to eat it.

Calvin hummed as he made his way back to shore. Brownie, his best friend and fishing partner, was with him in the small, dirty boat. Calvin was in high spirits. There was a lot to be thankful for. His wife's eye surgery had been a success and she was now seeing well, tomorrow was his wedding day, and they had hauled in a good catch, enough fish to add to the menu along with the curry goat, fried chicken, rice and peas and potato salad to feed his guests tomorrow.

Lenky had promised to attend. He was feeling good about that. He liked the gangster. Lenky had a good heart underneath it all. His wedding gift was a three day stay for the newlyweds in the honeymoon suite at a couples resort in Negril. Calvin really appreciated the gesture.

He wasn't stupid though. Very few things in life were free. And one day, Lenky would want something in return. And there was no way that he would be able to say no, not after all that Lenky had done for him.

Laura sighed contentedly as she padded downstairs in her Burberry robe. She had just taken a shower after her torrid after-lunch session with Steel. The sex had been great. Jerome's shoes were impossible to walk in but Steel had reminded her in fine style that he was no slouch in the lay-the-pipe-down department. A trip to New York after she got the abortion was definitely on the cards. She opened the fridge and extracted a bottle of beer for Steel and some juice for herself.

She paused when she heard the sound of a powerful engine in the driveway. Her heartbeat became irregular and her knees turned to jelly.

No way! He's supposed to be Montego Bay!

But there was no mistaking it. She knew the sound of her husband's Lincoln Navigator. Stark raving fear spurred her into action. She left the juice and beer on the kitchen counter and ran as fast as she could upstairs.

A professional hundred meter sprinter would've been proud of her.

CHAPTER 26

"Damn...that was so good ladies...I won't be able to move for a week," Jerome groaned, finally pushing his plate away.

"Thanks but you didn't have to eat so much baby," Angela responded, shaking her head in amusement. The men had dived into the curried shrimp, fried chicken, potato salad, white rice, and steamed vegetables, and did not come up for air except to ask for seconds. A lot of food had been cooked, and it was all gone, which pleased the two chefs to no end.

Jerome slapped her playfully on the butt and went outside to stretch his legs and try to walk some of the food off. He was so full that he was uncomfortable. Gunner grabbed some marijuana from off the cutting board and followed him outside.

They walked down to the beach as they rolled their joints.

"Seems like Lenky has gone back to Kingston," Gunner commented.

"Yeah," Jerome agreed. They had not seen him or any of the members of his crew since Friday. Jerome wondered what was going to happen when he got back to Kingston. Would he and Lenky ever speak again? Would Lenky try to make a move on Gunner before Gunner leaves to go home on Wednesday? Lenky was the type to hold a grudge so anything was possible.

Jerome's phone beeped in his pocket. He took it out and checked it. It was a text message from Amelia letting him know that she was home in New Jersey and thanking him for fulfilling her fantasy and giving her the most amazing sex that she had ever experienced. She also told him to be sure to link her anytime that he was in the tri-state area.

Jerome smiled and slipped the phone back into his pocket.

More than likely he would never see her again.

"Steel! My fucking husband just pulled up! If he sees you we're both fucking dead!" Laura whispered hoarsely, her chest heaving from her uncharacteristic run and the possible consequences of her actions.

Steel sprang up from the loveseat.

"What! Fuck!" he exclaimed.

Laura took a deep breath to calm down. She wasn't going out like this. She had to do *something.*

"Grab your clothes and go inside the closet and pull the door shut. Stay there until I come back," Laura instructed.

Steel stood there looking at her like she was crazy.

"Go!" Laura said forcefully, giving him a push. "I'll be back."

Laura pulled the bedroom door shut behind her, placed a smile on her face and headed down the stairs, her heart racing with each step.

"Honey I'm home," she heard Lenky call out, sounding very pleased with himself.

"I don't know what I'm going to do when Gunner goes home on Wednesday," Lola sighed. "I'm going to miss him so much. The last few days have been like a dream. And I don't want to wake up."

Angela nodded solemnly. She could relate. Jerome would be leaving for England in a week and a half and she was dreading it. She missed him already.

"I also have this fear Angie...suppose this is all a joke to him, just having a good time...and when he goes back he forgets about me? I mean...everything happened so fast, you know. It's almost unreal."

Angela shook her head emphatically as she sat up on the bed. They were in Lola and Gunner's room, chilling on the bed.

"That's not gonna happen Lola. Gunner loves you to death. Even Stevie Wonder could see that. Love has no time frame. You could be with someone for years and never feel for them what you feel for somebody else in just a few days. Gunner is serious about you...you have nothing to worry about."

Lola smiled weakly.

She sure hoped that Angela was right.

Or she was in for some serious heartache.

"Hey baby!" Laura gushed, moving quickly down the stairs towards Lenky who was standing in the middle of the expansive living room, holding a gift bag in his right hand. Blacka and Ping Pong sat down on the sofa and Blacka turned on the TV.

"Slow down baby," Lenky chided gently, thoroughly enjoying the fact that his wife was so happy to see him. She hugged him tightly and kissed him deeply. Wow. Laura could be very loving when she wanted to but this was something new. Maybe a positive spin-off of her having his seed inside her belly. He could definitely get used to this.

His heart swelled with passion along with his dick as he returned her kiss ardently.

Laura finally allowed them to come up for air, and looked over at Blacka and Ping Pong who were watching them and smirking.

"You guys need to go somewhere...I need some privacy with my husband," she told them, her flushed face and pouty lips telling them exactly what she had in mind.

Lenky almost came in his pants.

Grinning, Blacka and Ping Pong told Lenky that they would see him later and left the house.

Laura pounced on Lenky the minute that the door closed behind them.

"I missed you so much baby," she cooed, urgently unbuckling his belt and pulling down his jeans. "I got so wet when I heard your voice. Touch me and see how wet I am..."

Lenky, breathing like there was precious little air in the room, tossed her gift bag onto the nearest sofa and pushed his hand through the slit in her robe. He touched her cleanly shaven mound. He groaned. Her pussy was hot and wet.

Laura squatted and drooled on his dick, stroking it as she licked his scrotum. She knew that she didn't have much time before he climaxed so she bent over the arm of the couch and lifted one leg.

"Fuck me baby!" she urged, looking back at him wantonly.

Lenky growled and shoved his dick inside her.

"Yes baby! Fuck me!" Laura told him as he grunted and climaxed, clutching her tightly as he filled her with his seed.

Sweet Jesus, that was a record, even for him, Laura mused in wonder. He had literally only gotten three strokes off.

Lenky staggered over to the couch with his pants at his ankles and sat down.

"Damn baby...that hit the spot."

He handed her the gift bag.

"Thanks baby," Laura said, as she excitedly removed the two packages from the bag. She didn't have to pretend this time. Her glee was real. Whatever the gifts were, she knew that she would not be disappointed. Lenky only bought the best for her. She opened the larger package first.

"Awww...thanks boo, this is hot," she said, kissing him on the cheek. She put the Louis Vuitton clutch aside and opened the small gift box.

"Oh my God...baby you're the best hubby ever," she cooed, slipping on the gorgeous bracelet. It was a perfect fit.

Lenky was grinning from ear to ear. He was extremely pleased at everything that had transpired since he got home. It was moments like this that he felt like the happiest man in the world.

"Let me show you my gratitude," Laura said, smiling devilishly as she bent over and scooped up his flaccid dick with her mouth. Keeping her hands on his thighs, she sucked him mercilessly, pursing her lips as she coaxed his orgasm to the surface. It took her less than two minutes. Lenky celebrated his orgasm by calling on the Lord as his wife swallowed his hot juices.

"Jesus...Christ..." Lenky continued to blaspheme, looking at Laura in a combination of awe, love, lust and appreciation. He had married well, a beautiful exciting wife who adored him. Sure they have had their fair share of problems, but they had emerged stronger than ever from their battles, and soon, they would have a child together, the icing on the cake.

"Go take a shower baby, I want us to go out to dinner," she told him.

Lenky rose and pulled up his jeans.

"Ok, where you want to go?"

"I want Japanese," she told him.

They then climbed the stairs, hugging each other.

CHAPTER 27

"Let's go, hurry!" Laura hissed, as she opened the closet door. If the situation wasn't so serious it would have been funny. Steel was fully dressed, crouched in the walk-in closet, looking like a cornered rat.

Steel didn't even ask any questions. He simply scurried behind Laura down the stairs, praying that he'd get out of this alive. He had heard stories about Laura's husband. That man was nothing to fuck with. Lenky's name rang bells from Kingston to New York to L.A. to Miami.

Laura opened the door and told him to stand out on the road close to the gate; she would call a cab for him. She closed the door and breathed a sigh of relief. She had pulled it off. She grabbed the cordless phone on the antique table that she had purchased in New York and quickly flipped through the yellow pages to find a cab company that was close to Cherry Gardens. A company called Always on Time was located in Manor Park. Perfect. She quickly dialed the number and told the dispatcher her address and that the person would be waiting outside by the gate.

Scorcher slinked back inside the kitchen. He had come into the main house to see if anyone was around as he wanted some marijuana to smoke and he was out, only to see Laura coming down the stairs with a man who looked like he was near death. Instinct had made him pull back and remain unseen. Then he had stood by the doorway and listened to Laura hurriedly give the man instructions and call a cab.

Scorcher leaned against the kitchen counter and stroked his goatee. There was no doubt as to what he had just witnessed but it was hard to believe. Did Laura really have some guy in the house and smuggle him outside without Lenky knowing? Scorcher shook his head and smiled wryly. Women were devious creatures. They never ceased to amaze him. That dick must be real good, for her to risk her life like that. Too bad she never gave him a shot. She didn't know what she was missing. Cooking wasn't the only thing that he was good at.

Lenky was a good man. He had hired him and taken him off the streets. And he was grateful. But

Lenky's wife was hotter than most of the women he saw in magazines. If he had a chance to fuck her he would do it without hesitation. He just might have gotten his chance. And also the chance to make some extra money. He was positive that Laura would do anything to keep Lenky from finding out that she was cheating on him.

Lenky was out of the shower and getting dressed when Laura went back upstairs to the master bedroom. He looked at her in surprise.

"How come you don't start get ready yet?" he asked, pulling on a pair of charcoal grey slacks.

"I went to get some juice and then Khianna called, so I was talking to her about something," Laura responded, going into the bathroom to put on some make-up.

"Hurry up babes, mi getting hungry now," Lenky said, selecting a black button down from the closet. The Japanese restaurant that he would be taking her to was very upscale and had a strict dress code, casually elegant, whatever the fuck that meant. He would much rather go to a regular restaurant or a sports bar, but his wife loved to dine at the finest restaurants.

"Ok baby," Laura called out from the bathroom as she applied some blush to her cheeks.

Twenty minutes later, with Laura in a sexy black Dolce & Gabbana dress with a gold zipper in the back, they made their way out to the truck. Laura figured that Steel must be gone by now. The dispatcher at the cab company had said that the cab would be there in fifteen minutes.

They climbed in Lenky's Lincoln Navigator and headed out. Laura couldn't believe it. Steel was still there. The damn cab hadn't arrived yet. Lenky frowned as he looked over at the suspicious-looking man standing close to his gate. He stopped and rolled the window down.

"Why are you standing by my gate?" he asked gruffly.

Steel looked at Lenky and tried to keep his cool. Where was the damn cab?

"I'm standing on the road, I thought this was a free country," Steel responded. Wrong answer. Lenky placed the vehicle in park and hopped out.

"Baby, no, let's just go," Laura pleaded.

Lenky ignored her and went over to Steel. He whipped out his licensed firearm and struck Steel hard on the forehead.

"Pussyhole, move from mi gate, 'bout free country. Get the fuck outta here!" Lenky thundered. Steel held his hands up in surrender and turned and walked away. Lenky kicked him in the ass for good measure. Steel didn't dare look at Laura. He had never been more embarrassed in his life. His forehead was cut. Blood was on his shirt. He walked slowly, hoping that the vehicle approaching was the cab.

Lenky got back inside his vehicle and drove slowly beside Steel.

"If I ever see you in this neighbourhood again, any where close to my house, I am going to kill you," Lenky told him.

Steel didn't respond or look at him and Lenky drove off.

Laura felt bad for Steel but it was better that had happened as opposed to being caught inside the house. They would've both been dead. That had been a close call. She would never entertain another man in her home again.

CHAPTER 28

"It has been real Mobay, but we gotta go," Angela quipped as they drove out of the villa and started the long drive back to Kingston. Everyone chuckled. It had been a great trip. One that would hold lots of good memories.

Angela's mobile rang. She checked the caller I.D. It was her mother.

"Hi mom," Angela said. "What's up?"

"Hey Angie, just checking if you and Jerome will be coming for dinner this evening." David, her husband, was looking at her expectantly from his perch on the couch where he was watching a football game. He was quite fond of Jerome and was hoping that he would come for dinner.

"Yeah sure...we'll have two friends with us though."

"No problem, about what time?"

"We'll be there at five," Angela told her.

"Ok then, see you later."

Dahlia put the phone down.

"They're coming for dinner at five and they'll be bringing a couple of friends," she informed David, making her way to the kitchen.

She took out a tray of mutton, deciding to add another meat to the menu. She thought about Sara as she began the dinner preparations. Sara wasn't home today, as was becoming the norm lately. She would disappear for hours on end without telling anyone where she was going or had been. Dahlia wanted to ask but was afraid of causing any friction. Sara didn't volunteer any information and she seemed to be ok, if reserved, so they let it be.

Dahlia wondered if she and Sara would ever be close again. Even when David was not speaking to Sara and she was not welcome at their home, a situation that had grieved her to no end, her and Sara had maintained a good relationship. Hopefully, after Sara had fully recovered from her traumatic experience, they would once again enjoy a tight relationship.

Only time would tell.

Lenky smiled as the Pastor, a thin elderly man who looked like a strong gust of wind could blow him away like a piece of paper, pronounced the bride and groom husband and wife. He reflected on his wedding day almost two years ago. It was an opulent affair, a stark contrast to the humble surroundings and guests of this one. The wedding ceremony was being held at the church Calvin used to attend as a boy, a concrete structure in dire need of paint.

No formal invitations had been issued, the close knit community knew that Calvin was getting married and almost everyone was there. Even Miss Mattie, one of the oldest women in the community who had not left her home in over three years – last time was a doctor's visit when her blood pressure was too high – was present. She was seated at the front, watching the proceedings keenly in a dress and hat that hadn't been in fashion since the 70s. Everyone couldn't hold inside the church, so some were by the windows and door looking in, and many others were content to mill about in the church yard, waiting for the best part of any wedding – the reception. Many had not cooked Sunday dinner, hoping to get enough to eat at the reception.

Calvin kissed his new wife and the guests applauded. A few minutes later, the smiling husband and wife then made their way slowly out of the church, to the sounds of the Mento band that was playing. The leader of the band was Calvin's cousin and was happy to play at the wedding free of cost.

The bride and groom rode to their home in Lenky's Lincoln Navigator, the first time either of them had ever been inside a luxury vehicle. Calvin thanked Lenky profusely for all of his help on the ride home. Lenky merely smiled magnanimously and told him it's all good, they would have a chat when he got back from his honeymoon.

Calvin wondered what that chat would entail. He knew that his wife wasn't too comfortable with Lenky being in their lives, being a notorious gangster and all, and though she was also grateful for all he had done for them, had wondered out loud on a few occasions why he was so nice to Calvin. What would he want in return?

He shrugged those thoughts aside and smiled at his wife. Today was a special day and he wasn't going to spend it dwelling on negative thoughts.

CHAPTER 29

Sara returned to the house at 6 p.m. She had spent the day with Derrick. They had a lovely picnic at Castleton Gardens and then watched a romantic comedy at his home when they got back to Kingston. The only reason that she had come home so early was because she was really horny and wanted to honour their agreement that they would wait a while before having sex.

If she had stayed Derrick would've been inside her right now. The thought made her seep moisture. Her panties were drenched. She was really anxious to experience what it was like making love to someone that she was truly in love with, and who was in love with her. She thought it was the final step in getting rid of the stain that those rapists had left on her womb.

She entered the living room and heard the cacophony of voices in the dining room. She could hear Jerome telling a joke and everyone was cracking up. *Not only a star football player and a stud, but also a comedian huh*, Sara mused sarcastically. She was tempted to just go to her room without saying good evening to anyone but decided against it though she badly wanted to remove her wet underwear.

"Hi honey," Dahlia said, when she entered the room. "Hungry?"

"No, Mother," Sara replied, looking around the table. She was shocked to see Gunner. Her mind flashed back to the fun weekend she had had with her friend Deborah, Gunner and Jerome in London.

"Hey Sara," Jerome said warmly.

"Hi Jerome, hey Gunner, how are you?" Sara said.

"You know Gunner?" Angela asked, surprised.

Yes I do sis, I had the time of my life in London fucking the shit out of Jerome at Gunner's apartment.

Aloud she responded, "Yeah, met him through a mutual friend in London."

She chatted with them for a bit and Gunner introduced her to Lola. Sara wondered what had become of Deborah but didn't ask. None of that stuff mattered any more. Not even Angela and Jerome being together had any effect.

She was over it all and wished them well. She was truly happy for the first time in a long time. She would go back to the apartment in Waterloo soon. She was ready to be back on her own. Being at home with her parents was starting to feel stifling.

She excused herself after a few minutes, telling them that she was tired.

She went inside her room and locked the door. She stripped down immediately and entered the shower.

She urgently needed to deal with the ache between her legs.

She switched on the flexible shower head and held it a few inches from her throbbing pussy.

The water, shooting forcefully through thirty tiny holes, stung her shaven mound pleasurably.

Her fingers took care of the rest.

Steel looked out the window as his flight took off. His first trip to his homeland in over five years had been an eventful one to say the least. He had thoroughly enjoyed the three nights of Reggae Sumfest that he had attended, but after what happened at Laura's home on Saturday, he was happy to see the back of Jamaica. Those few hours of pleasure with Laura had almost turned out to be his last. His six year old daughter had almost lost her father. The thought made him shiver. Laura had called him yesterday in the afternoon to check up on him and promised to make it up to him when she visits New York in a few weeks.

He would definitely hold her to that. Make her spend some of Lenky's money on him.

That would help to put a band aid on his wounded ego.

Monday flew by quickly for Jerome. He spent the first half of the day working on his conditioning, then had a meeting with a local designer who wanted him to model his clothes at an upcoming celebrity charity fashion show, and he also made some important calls, one to his new boss at Manchester FC to follow up on his housing situation – everything was indeed in place for his arrival – and one to a doctor that he knew well and could trust, to set up an appointment for Laura's abortion.

Then it was off to an evening out for the two couples. They dined at a plush Indian eatery in Manor Park before going to the movies to see an action flick. Neither Angela nor Lola was into chick flicks, much to the delight of their men.

Bishop and his crew were no longer with them. Bishop's little brother was killed last night in an alleged shootout with the police and Bishop had headed over to his stronghold the minute he got the call.

Gunner hoped that his last two days in the country would be drama free but he was armed and prepared just in case Lenky still had a bug up his ass. He sincerely hoped nothing jumped off though as he wouldn't want anything to happen to Lola because of him. He had said as much to her but she had dismissed his fears, saying that she would be right by his side up until he went to the airport on Wednesday.

After the movies, Jerome dropped them off at the hotel and then went home with Angela. Tomorrow night was Gunner's final night so they would be doing it all over again, but would be going clubbing after dinner this time.

CHAPTER 30

Laura got up at 10 a.m., showered and went downstairs. The helper, who was dusting the furniture in the living room, asked her what she wanted for breakfast. Laura told her to have the chef prepare an omelette with toast. She would be out by the pool. Armed with a novel about a shopaholic from New York, she went out to the pool and made herself comfortable on the lounge chair.

She was in a good mood. Things were looking up. Jerome had sent her a text last night informing her that he had set up an appointment for her to see a doctor on Wednesday, so that problem was well on its way to being solved; she had fucked Steel in her home and gotten away with it, which had provided a thrill that was so intense that she had forgotten how scared she was and she would be moving forward with plans to open her luxury clothing store by Christmas.

Life was good. Her mind ran on her husband. She wondered why he had left the house so early this morning. She had gotten up to pee at 5:30 a.m. and he wasn't home. A shadow loomed over her. It was Scorcher, the chef, holding a tray with her omelette, toast, orange juice and coffee.

She gestured for him to put it on the table and got up to sit at the table. She took a sip of her coffee and noticed that he was still standing there.

"That will be all," she said airily, dismissing him. To her chagrin, he grabbed a seat instead and sat down across from her.

"Mi need to talk to yuh 'bout something," he said, smiling smugly.

"Look, Fire, Pepper, whatever your name is, I don't converse with the help while I eat. Whatever it is you can talk about it when you come back to fetch the tray," she responded.

"Mi name is Scorcher and it can't wait. Mi know that yuh did have a man inside the house Saturday... now de question is...what will you give me so that I don't tell yuh husband?"

Laura's eyes widened in shock.

Lenky belched loudly in appreciation of Jada's delicious cooking. He had just wolfed down a meal of calalloo, fried plantains, fried breadfruit, Johnny cakes and chocolate tea. He had stopped at Jada's for a late breakfast after taking care of some business at the airport. A shipment of six kilos of cocaine was sent off this morning to Eduardo in Miami, and he had just gotten a call that it had arrived undetected and was in the process of being cleared by their contact in customs. He would be making a clear one hundred and thirty thousand US dollars after expenses, off this shipment.

A wonderful way to start the day.

Laura recovered quickly. She calmly ate a piece of her omelette and looked at him steadily. He must have somehow seen her when she was getting Steel out of the house, or saw when he came there, or heard them fucking. It didn't matter. The danger was over. He had no proof. Sure Lenky saw a guy outside the gate but it would be this idiot's word against hers, and there was no way in hell that Lenky would believe that she had so brazenly cheated on him in his own home. His love for her and his ego wouldn't entertain the thought. He would probably kill Scorcher for coming to him with something like that.

"Even if that was true asshole, good luck with convincing my husband. You have no proof," she sneered.

Scorcher was taken aback. He hadn't expected her to respond like this. He frowned as he contemplated her words. Reluctantly, he had to admit that she was right. How could he prove it? And to go to Lenky with such an accusation without proof would be a death wish. He suddenly wished that he hadn't said anything to her. What was going to happen now?

He smiled nervously.

"Yuh right...mi can't prove it...so we will just leave it at that," he said, rising.

Laura smirked but did not respond.

That's what you think asshole.

She watched as he ambled off.

The nerve of this punk trying to blackmail her.

He was going to pay for that, and pay dearly.

Lenky went home at 5 p.m. He was looking forward to spending some time with his wife, as he had been on the road since the crack of dawn. He entered through the front door with Blacka and Ping Pong behind him.

"Don't touch me! Don't fucking touch me! Are you crazy?" Lenky heard Laura screaming frantically. Shocked, he rushed inside the kitchen with Blacka and Ping Pong on his heels.

Laura was pushing and slapping Scorcher, screaming obscenities and crying. Lenky grabbed and held her, hugging her to him. Blacka and Ping Pong stood at either side of Scorcher, waiting to hear what had happened.

"Baby, calm down, what the fuck is going on?" Lenky demanded.

"Boss, mi-" Scorcher said, attempting to explain.

"Shut your mouth!" Lenky thundered, glaring at him. "I asked my wife, not you!"

Laura composed herself and used a paper towel to wipe her eyes.

"I came into the kitchen to get a snack and he-he-he came behind me and pressed me against the counter, telling me that I was sexy and that you alone couldn't manage all of this ass, so I pushed him and slapped his face and that's when you came in," Laura sniffed.

Lenky's blood turned to ice. He whipped out his gun and pointed it at Scorcher's head, as Scorcher, the realization of what Laura had done making him weak in the bowels, opened his mouth to speak, his mouth moving like a mime, no words coming out.

Lenky changed his mind and put the gun down on the kitchen counter. He grabbed a knife instead and stepped up to Scorcher.

"You disrespectful, ungrateful fucker!" he hissed, and slashed Scorcher's throat. Blood sprayed liberally, drenching Blacka and Ping Pong, and ruined Lenky's white shirt. Lenky kept on slashing, slicing Scorcher all over, and when Scorcher fell to the ground, his body jerking like he was possessed, Lenky bent over him and stabbed him repeatedly. He didn't stop when Scorcher stopped moving. He kept on stabbing until his arm was tired.

Laura had seen violent acts before, but nothing compared to the viciousness that she had just witnessed. She turned to run to the bathroom to throw up. She didn't make it.

Even Blacka and Ping Pong, who had both taken several lives in their long criminal career, were shaken. It wasn't that Lenky had killed Scorcher; it was *how* he killed him.

Lenky rose slowly, looking like a survivor from a horror movie. He looked down on his handiwork, his face filled with contempt.

He spat on the body.

"Dispose of the garbage," he said as he turned and walked away.

Vomit was all over the living room carpet and he could hear Laura in one of the bathrooms downstairs crying and throwing up.

He didn't go to her.

He went upstairs to clean up.

"To us," Jerome said, raising his glass of champagne.

"To us," everyone said in a chorus, touching their glasses in unison.

The two couples were dining under the stars at DiFara's, an upscale Italian restaurant located on Belmont Road in New Kingston. All dressed in black, they were seated at a cozy table for four, dining on freshly prepared meatballs tossed in a Napoli sauce with classic spaghetti pasta, Arborio rice served with a sauce of wild mushrooms, parmesan and spinach, and herb encrusted salmon served on a bed of spring onion mash and creamy dill sauce.

After dinner the fun would continue with a stop at Privilege Playground, the most exclusive club in Kingston. It was so exclusive that only premium liquor was available there and all the waitresses looked like beauty contestants.

"Ahem," Gunner said, clearing his throat.

He looked at Lola. He was smiling but his eyes were serious. He pushed his chair back and got up. He then got down on one knee beside Lola's chair. She covered her mouth with one hand, her pretty eyes suddenly filled with tears. Was he about to do what she thought he was going to do? She felt like she was going to have a heart attack.

"Baby, I've only known you for nine days, but it may as well be nine years as I feel like I've known you forever. I never believed in the concept of a soul mate until I met you. I never thought in a million years that I could love another human being the way I love you. You are my world, baby. I can't imagine my life without you in it. I want to grow old with you. I want you to be the mother of my children. Lola, will you marry me?"

Lola wasn't just teary eyed anymore. She was crying now, hard. Joyful sobs that wracked her body as she nodded vigourously, watching in disbelief as he slipped a gorgeous ring onto her finger.

She hugged Gunner fiercely and gave him a kiss.

"Oh my God...congratulations Lola...that was the most romantic thing I've ever seen..." Angela cooed, teary-eyed as well, as she gave Lola a hug.

Jerome grinned and shook Gunner's hand. He had also bought a ring at the jewelry store that Gunner bought his. A very expensive but understated engagement ring. Angela would love it. Gunner had asked him if he was going to propose tonight as well but he had told him no. Tonight was Gunner's night. And Lola's. He didn't know as yet when he was going to propose to Angela, but when the moment was right, he would.

Angela accompanied Lola to the restroom to wash her face and reapply her make-up. When they returned to the table, Angela gave her camera to the waiter who waited their table and asked him sweetly to take a group photo of them. They smiled as he snapped the picture, the joy of the night evident in their faces and body language.

It was a good thing that Angela had thought to capture the moment.

It would be the last time that all four of them would be together.

CHAPTER 31

Laura groaned as she glanced at the time on her mobile. It was 1 a.m. and despite her fatigue, more mental than physical, she was unable to sleep. She hadn't known what she expected to happen when she set up Scorcher, but she had not envisioned the carnage that she had witnessed. A man had been butchered like a pig right before her very eyes, because of her. She was sick to her stomach. The guilt of sending an innocent man to such a brutal death was weighing heavily on her soul.

She had prayed to God several times since it happened, but the burden had not lessened, it had intensified as the hours wore on. She could see Scorcher's face, eyes wide in disbelief at the lies she had told on him, a mask of terror when Lenky held the gun on him, the blood spraying when Lenky slit his throat, the stunning savageness of the multiple slashes and stabs, even when he was dead.

She couldn't eat. She couldn't sleep. She couldn't function. There was no way that she could ever set foot back inside the kitchen. She thought about the abortion that she was going to do tomorrow. More death. The thought made her stomach churn. She felt nauseas but she knew from the last two trips to the bathroom that there was nothing left inside her to throw up.

She closed her eyes and opened them back quickly in fright.

Scorcher, blood spraying from his neck, was pointing at her and screaming 'murderer!' Shaking, she pulled the covers up to her neck. Lenky was right beside her fast asleep. She wished that she could snuggle up against him but she couldn't. She didn't feel comfortable with his hands touching her. The same hands that had mercilessly slaughtered Scorcher.

She wondered how long it would be before things returned to normal.

She wondered if they ever would.

The foursome decided to call it a night at 1:30 a.m. They were having a great time but between dinner and the club, Angela had exceeded her planned drinking limit and was feeling the effects. Not good seeing as she had a full day at work starting at 8:30. They trooped out of the club, laughing at Lola's champagne-fueled plan of getting married in a white two piece bikini set – in a church. They climbed into the SUV and Jerome did a tricky maneuver to get out of their parking spot as an inconsiderate person had not parked properly beside them. The large Dodge Ram was partially blocking their vehicle.

He made it without scratching the vehicle, to the semi-drunken cheers of his passengers and headed down Knutsford Boulevard.

Lola, snuggled up against Gunner in the back-seat, looked at him solemnly.

"You'll never love another woman, baby," she told him.

Gunner smiled at her, wondering why she looked so serious.

"Well it's a good thing I won't have to," he responded, giving her a peck on the lips. "Together for ever, babe."

They glanced at a cop car that had pulled over by the curb close to the entrance of the hotel. The two cops were talking to a young woman who seemed to be a prostitute, if her outfit was anything to go by. She was bent over by the driver window of the cop car, her short red dress resting on the top of her ample ass which was on display for anyone driving by to see.

Angela shook her head in disgust. Jerome turned into the hotel and pulled up in front of the lobby.

"Ok mate, see you later," Gunner said, giving Jerome a pound. "Bye Angie."

"Bye Gunner, Lola, love you guys," Angela said, as Lola kissed her cheek from behind.

Gunner exited the vehicle and held Lola's hand to help her out. They walked slowly towards the lobby as Gunner fished in his pants pocket for the key to the suite. He took it out and it fell. Two shots rang out in the still of the night as he stooped to pick it up.

He froze in horror as Lola fell to the ground beside him with a dull thud.

CHAPTER 32

"Bloodclaat!" Ping Pong cursed, realizing that he had missed Gunner and shot his girl instead. His gun was now jammed and Blacka was shouting for him to come on. He stuck the gun inside his waistband and jumped on the back of the powerful motorcycle. Blacka revved the engine and sped off, crashing headfirst into the cops, who upon hearing the shots, had abandoned their negotiations with the prostitute and sped inside the hotel while calling for backup.

Blacka went through the windscreen of the cop car headfirst, showering the two cops with broken glass. Ping Pong was thrown high into the air and fell hard to the ground, breaking his right arm in two places, the impact jarring the jammed bullet free. The gun went off, turning his groin into a gaping hole.

His scream was inhumane.

"Jesus Christ," Jerome whispered, holding his head in agony, as he walked slowly over to Gunner, who was sitting in a pool of blood, with Lola's lifeless body cradled in his arms. The pain evident on his handsome face was indescribable.

"Oh my God, no, no, oh God," Angela, though Jerome had told her to stay in the vehicle until he found out was happening, sobbed as she took in the heart-breaking scene, holding on to Jerome for support.

They had heard the shots seconds after driving off. Jerome had stopped suddenly, and when he didn't hear any more shots, had placed the vehicle in park and told Angela to stay put.

Sirens blared, signaling the arrival of more police officers. The security guards at the hotel had locked the doors to the lobby and were out front with the night manager, who wondered balefully why this had to happen on his shift.

The senior detective on the scene, a burly veteran cop with a gravelly voice, recognized Jerome and asked if he knew what happened. Jerome tearfully recounted the last ten minutes.

When showed Ping Pong's dead body, he identified him, and told the cop who Ping Pong was working for, and gave him the background information, establishing a motive for the shooting. There was no way that he would protect Lenky, knowing that he was behind this gruesome act. An innocent life was lost. And for what? Petty jealousy.

The cop nodded grimly as he took notes. Lenky. Damn he hated that man. He could have busted him many times for various offences but Lenky had friends in high places, including his superior. But all things, good and bad, must come to an end. And Lenky's criminal reign of impunity was very close to an end, for more reasons than one.

Blacka was on the ground in handcuffs, bleeding from a head wound and lacerations to the face and neck. The police, having searched and found an illegal firearm on him, were taking their own sweet time to take him to the hospital for treatment. They wouldn't mind if he died before he got there. Treating him would be a waste of taxpayers' money.

The detective thanked Jerome for his help, and then interviewed three hotel employees, including a security guard that had witnessed the shooting. Gunner, still in shock, refused to let go of Lola's body. The police, in sympathy, and because Gunner and the dead female were good friends of Jerome, did not force the issue. They allowed him to hold the body until the ambulance arrived to take it away.

"She's dead because of me Jerome," Gunner whispered hoarsely, as Jerome knelt beside him, trying to get him to let go of Lola. The cops had taken all their notes, done their interviews, and the hotel management was anxious to have the body removed.

"I might as well had pulled the trigger my fucking self...my baby...my heartbeat is gone...oh God."

The pain in Gunner's voice made Jerome wince.

"What am I going to do without her Jerome? Fucking hell man, I can't believe she's gone," Gunner sobbed.

"They have to remove her body," Jerome said gently, his arm around Gunner's shoulders.

Gunner used his sleeve to wipe his eyes and looked at his dead fiancé for several more seconds before closing her eyes with a trembling hand. He then tenderly moved her torso from off of his lap and laid her on the ground.

Jerome helped him up and led him inside. Angela told Jerome to wait inside the lobby, and went over to the SUV which was still idling a few feet away. She climbed in and parked it, then went into the lobby. Jerome and Gunner were standing by the elevator waiting for her. When she got to them they took the elevator and went up to Gunner's suite.

Gunner went straight into the bathroom and closed the door. Jerome and Angela sat on the bed beside each other and she rested her head on his shoulder. After a few moments they could hear the shower running.

The water did little to drown out the sounds of agony coming from the bathroom.

CHAPTER 33

L aura had just fallen asleep from sheer exhaustion when Lenky's mobile rang insistently, waking her up. Cursing under her breath, she groggily picked the phone up, shook Lenky awake, and gave it him.

"Your phone won't stop ringing," Laura said, thoroughly annoyed. It was 3:30 a.m. She had only dozed off for about fifteen minutes. She turned her back to Lenky and closed her eyes. At least Scorcher wasn't pointing at her and screaming murderer anymore. Maybe he was tired too.

"Hello," Lenky said gruffly.

"Rassclaat," he said, after listening for a few minutes. It was a young police officer that was on his payroll calling to let him know about the debacle involving Blacka and Ping Pong at the Barcelona Court hotel.

He climbed out of bed and went out to the balcony. "Alright, later."

He shook his head in disgust as he terminated the call. It appeared that the only way to get anything done right these days was to do it yourself. Blacka and Ping Pong had made a complete hash of killing Gunner. They had killed his bitch instead, Ping Pong was dead, having shot his own dick off; and Blacka was in the hospital under police guard.

That's why he needed Calvin as his right hand man. Strong, reliable and loyal. He was going to meet with him as soon as he got back from his honeymoon tomorrow. And he was not going to take no for an answer. He liked Calvin, and was happy to have helped him out, but that was the way it worked. *I scratch your back, you scratch mine. Nothing in life is free.*

He looked over his shoulder at his wife wrapped up in the sheets. Scorcher's death had shaken her up really badly. Well, she would get over it eventually. Scorcher had violated his wife in his own home. Disrespected his trust and his kindness. He deserved what he got. And that's all there was to it.

He went back inside the bedroom and climbed into bed. There was nothing to worry about. Yeah, they had Blacka in custody but he wouldn't dare implicate Lenky and between Lenky's high priced lawyer and his police connections, Blacka would soon be a free man.

Lenky closed his eyes and went back to sleep.

Angela didn't go to work. She would not have been able to function. She called her assistant and told her to reschedule her appointments for the day. She and Jerome had spent the night in Gunner's suite, not wanting him to be by himself. He had gotten out of the shower after what seemed like an eternity, two hours to be exact, and had sat in the lounge chair on the balcony all night, nursing a bottle of Hennessy, which he drank straight.

Jerome and Angela had eventually fallen asleep, on Gunner's bed, though there was another bedroom in the suite. When they woke up at 7, Gunner was fast asleep on the balcony, drunk to the world. They lifted him and placed him in the bed. He did not stir.

Not feeling well, Angela asked Jerome to take her to see her doctor. They went home, showered and changed, then drove to Seymour Place where Angela's doctor, an affable man with a fondness for telling corny jokes, was located.

Jerome's phone rang while Angela was inside the doctor's office.

He frowned as he looked at the caller ID. He didn't recognize the number and was tempted not to answer it. He had been getting a lot of calls all morning, as there were two rumors going around: that he had gotten shot and the other, which the mere thought of it had chilled his soul, that his girlfriend had been killed. He was sick of it. Against his better judgment, he answered the call.

"Jerome, its Laura...I left my cell phone at home when I was rushing out. I'm at the doctor's office. I go in to see him in five minutes. Are you on your way?"

Shit! Jerome cursed inwardly. He had completely forgotten that Laura's appointment to have the abortion was this morning. He had promised to accompany her. Well, there was nothing he could do about that now. He simply couldn't make it.

"I won't be able to make it Laura...it's a bit crazy around here right now. Your fucking husband tried to kill Gunner last night and ended up killing his fiancé instead," Jerome told her bluntly.

"What!" Laura exclaimed.

"Oh you didn't know? Yeah, he sent Blacka and Ping Pong to do the job...Ping Pong is dead and Blacka is in police custody."

"Fuck!" Laura rubbed her temple. What in the world was going on? The last twenty four hours had been way too crazy. She felt like she was caught up in a bad nightmare that just kept getting worse. That must've been why Lenky's phone had been ringing like crazy in the wee hours of the morning.

Laura sighed in frustration. She was really looking forward to Jerome coming and giving her support through the process. Now she would have to face it alone. She was tired, stressed and scared, and she really needed him right now. She had left her truck at Khianna's home and taken a cab to the doctor's office. Lenky would have been suspicious if he saw her vehicle at home and she wasn't there. How was she going to get back to Khianna's? The doctor had told her that someone should accompany her so that she could get home safely as she would be very weak and in a lot of discomfort after the procedure.

She didn't want Khianna all up in her business but she had no choice.

"Ok fuck it, I'll talk to you later," she told Jerome and hung up.

"May I make another call please?" she asked the receptionist.

"Dr. Burford is ready for you," the receptionist responded.

"I need to make this call before I go in," Laura explained. "My ride home won't be able to make it."

The receptionist nodded and told her to make it quick.

"Sophia!" Lenky bellowed for the cleaning lady, as he went down the stairs. He was famished, and with Scorcher dead and Blacka in police custody, she would have to be the one to prepare him breakfast. Laura had left a note on the bedside table saying that she had a hair and nails appointment and would see him later. Not that she was of any use in the kitchen.

The remaining members of his inner circle would be coming by the house for a meeting at 11. It was now 9 a.m.

"Yes sir?" Sophia said, entering the living room.

"You can cook?" Lenky asked gruffly.

"Yes, sir," she responded, wondering where Scorcher was. She was scared to death of Lenky and wouldn't want to make him something and it wasn't to his satisfaction.

He decided to keep it simple seeing as he was so hungry.

"I want a fried egg, sausages, fried plantain with four slices of bread and some orange juice. Bring it out by de pool. An' mek it snappy."

Sophia nodded and hurried to the kitchen.

Lenky was heading out to the pool when he noticed Laura's Blackberry on the couch.

He picked it up and carried it with him.

CHAPTER 34

"Another day of rest and you'll be fine Angie," Dr. Shields announced, smiling fondly. He had been Angela's doctor since she was ten years old and he had watched her grow into a fine young lady. "Just mental exhaustion and stress. Nothing rest won't cure."

Angela sat up and adjusted her blouse. She was surprised to hear that was all there was to it. Her body was feeling weird. She got up from off the examination table and sat at his desk.

"By the way," Dr. Shields continued casually, "you're pregnant."

Angela gasped and her hands unconsciously went to her tender breasts.

"I hope that's good news," he said, smiling broadly.

Angela tried to hold the tears back. The last couple of months had been an incredible ride. Everything had happened so fast. Meeting Jerome, his determined courting, their incredible connection, and now she was going to have his baby. Wow.

"It's great news," she whispered. She had lost a good friend to murder mere hours ago, and now she had just learnt that she was going to be a mother.

What an emotional roller coaster.

Lenky sat down on the lounge chair, the large umbrella shielding him from the searing mid-morning sun. Laura never left the house without her mobile. She must have been in quite a rush this morning. He decided to go through her phone. He clicked on the message icon so he that could see her text messages. He frowned when he saw Jerome's name. What the fuck was Jerome's number doing in his wife's phone and why were they texting each other?

He opened the messages and stiffened like a corpse. He blinked and read them again. And again. He simply could not believe what he was seeing. Laura was pregnant for Jerome. Not him. Laura did not have a hair and nails appointment. She was gone to abort the baby in her stomach. So many different emotions were assaulting Lenky simultaneously that he felt like he was going to explode. Tears rolled down his cheeks and his chest heaved mightily as his brain struggled to process the unbelievable discovery.

His wife and former best friend had played him for a fool. He had never felt so hurt and betrayed in his entire life.

226

He trembled with rage.

They were going to die.

Slowly and painfully.

"Police! Police! Hands in the air!" came the shout as several police officers, some in plain clothes, all with guns drawn, swarmed the pool area.

Sophia, who was on her way out there to bring Lenky his breakfast, screamed and dropped the tray.

Lenky got up and ran inside.

"Don't shoot!" the American DEA agent in charge of the apprehension team commanded. "I want the bastard alive if possible."

He signaled and they entered the house in search of Lenky.

Khianna helped Laura out of the doctor's office. She was shocked when she saw Laura's disheveled appearance. Laura looked like she had just had a fight and got her ass royally kicked. Laura groaned as she got into the passenger side of her SUV. Khianna could drive but did not own a car, so when Laura had called her to come down to the doctor's office, she had driven Laura's truck.

Khianna drove the short distance to the pharmacy which was on the same complex, and leaving Laura inside the vehicle, went in there to fill Laura's prescription. Laura moaned, wishing Khianna would hurry up so that she could start taking her medication and go to sleep. She was experiencing severe abdominal pain, had a slight fever and was bleeding.

She looked out at a little girl standing in front of the pharmacy, smiling and eating candy, while a woman, presumably her mother, chatted away on her cell phone. She hoped that the little girl would never have to go through what she just did. Mercifully, Khianna returned quickly and they headed to Khianna's home.

Laura wondered if Lenky would buy her story that the stress of witnessing him brutally kill Scorcher had caused her to have a miscarriage.

She prayed that he would.

It was the only one that she had to sell.

"I'm going back to the apartment tomorrow," Sara said, looking at her parents. She had told them that she needed to speak with them after breakfast, so the three of them gathered on the patio.

"Are you sure you're ready to be alone, dear?" Dahlia asked gently.

"Yes, mother."

Dahlia knew that tone all too well. Sara's mind was made up. David appraised his youngest daughter silently. He didn't mind, the sooner the better. Having her around on a daily basis brought back too many memories.

"I have a surprise for you," he told her, getting up to go into his study.

He returned with an envelope which he handed to Sara.

Sara opened it nonchalantly.

Inside was a check for two hundred and fifty thousand dollars, and the title for the Waterloo apartment.

"I knew you would be ready to leave the nest again soon, so I decided to give you a little something to help make the road ahead a bit smoother," David said, smiling broadly.

"Thank you," Sara said quietly. "I appreciate it."

If David was expecting a hug or an excited show of gratitude, he was sorely disappointed. No amount of material gifts could erase what he had done to her. But she wasn't stupid. She wasn't going to refuse the gesture and cut off her nose to spite her face. The apartment was at a prime location and though it was small, would fetch a tidy sum on the market. She would sell it when she and Derrick got married and started living together.

She looked at her mother and saw a sad understanding in her eyes. And at that moment, Sara realized without a doubt that her mother knew what her father had been doing to her all those years. How could she have stayed silent? Allowed it to continue?

Feeling the tears on their way, Sara excused herself and went to her room.

She locked the door and collapsed on the bed.

She cried like a baby.

Jerome got up and went over to Angela as soon as she entered the reception area.

He stood beside her as she paid her bill to one of the nurses at the front desk. They didn't speak until they got outside.

They walked to the truck with their arms around each other.

"The doctor says I'm basically ok, that I just need to rest," she told him. "I was just basically shell-shocked and stressed about what happened to poor Lola."

Jerome kissed her forehead.

"That's great, baby," he said, and opened the door for her. She went in and sat down, savouring the news that she had for him.

He climbed in and gunned the engine.

"Umm baby," Angela said. She couldn't hold it a moment longer though she was a tad bit nervous at what his reaction might be.

"Hmmm?" Jerome murmured, looking behind him as he began to reverse out of the parking spot.

"I'm pregnant."

Jerome braked suddenly and put the vehicle in park.

His handsome features broke out into a wide smile.

He reached over and pulled her to him.

They had a long, sweet kiss, ignoring the insistent horn of the angry driver that Jerome was blocking.

CHAPTER 35

Lenky reached the top of the stairs and rushed into the master bedroom, locking the door behind him. He was having a hard time comprehending how his entire world had been turned upside down in mere minutes. What the hell was the police doing here? Why hadn't he gotten a warning from the cops on his payroll about it? That could only mean one thing. They didn't know. This operation was clearly coming straight from the top.

Sweating profusely, he grabbed the cordless phone and frantically dialed his lawyer's number as he went inside the closet and retrieved his Heckler and Koch MP5 submachine gun. It was already fully loaded. He grabbed two extra clips and stuck them in his pockets.

Until he had an idea what this was about, he was not going to go quietly, if at all. Tears ran down his face at the possibility of not getting to have his revenge on Jerome and his bitch of a wife.

The lawyer's secretary answered the phone.

"I need to speak with Mr. Carson immediately," Lenky breathed, his heart accelerating as he heard multiple footsteps coming up the stairs.

"He's in a meeting, sir, and cannot be disturbed. Would you like to leave a message?"

"Bitch I need to talk to him now!" Lenky thundered. "This is a fucking emergency. Tell him Lenky is on the phone."

The secretary hung up on him. Lenky cursed and was about to redial the number when he heard a bull horn.

"Everton Bell, also known as Lenky, we have a warrant here for your arrest for conspiracy to traffic and distribute over 600 kilos of cocaine and over 5000 pounds of marijuana in the United States over a five year period. You are to be extradited to the United States where you will be arraigned for your crimes. Your friend Eduardo in Miami has been very cooperative in our investigation."

The man paused to let that sink in before he continued in his nasal American accent.

"The house is surrounded. You cannot escape. You have exactly one minute to surrender before we come in there and get you."

Lenky's brain was churning. What the fuck? Eduardo had turned State's evidence against him? That piece of shit. The Feds must have gotten to him and he gave him up to help shave some time off his sentence. Whatever happened to honour among thieves?

It was every man for himself these days, Lenky mused bitterly. They clearly had an airtight case to come at him like this. Lenky did the math mentally. They must have missed out on a few shipments as he was sure that he had shipped more than 600 kilos over that period.

He was clutching the gun so tightly that his knuckles hurt. He had seen other drug barons get life in prison for much lesser quantities. They were going to throw the book at him. He would spend the rest of his life in Federal prison. No fucking way. If only he could get out of the house. He could survive on the run. He had enough raw cash at different locations to help him get out of the country.

A canister of tear gas was thrown into the bedroom through the door leading out to the balcony, breaking him out of his reverie. He pulled his t-shirt up over his nose and kicked the can back out to the balcony and locked the door.

He turned back around just in time to see his bedroom door flattened by an explosion. Screaming like a maniac, he fired at the open space which was now filled with tear gas. He fired until his clip was empty.

Shaking with adrenaline, and coughing from the tear gas, he backed up towards the balcony door, inserting a fresh clip.

An agent, positioned on a branch of the apple tree in the back yard, several meters away from the pool, took aim with his rifle and fired.

The shot connected with the back of Lenky's head, blowing it to pieces.

CHAPTER 36

Gunner was still in bed when Jerome got back to the hotel, and let himself into Gunner's suite. He had taken the room key so that he wouldn't have any problems getting into the suite. He had dropped Angela off at her apartment, and told her to get some rest until he swung by later.

Jerome stood and looked at his best friend. Not even in his sleep was he getting any peace. He still wore a pained expression on his face. Jerome sat on the bed beside Gunner's sleeping form.

His heart went out to Gunner. He couldn't imagine losing Angela at all, much less under such heinous circumstances. The thought of it made him sick to his heart. And now she was going to be the mother of his child. Though marrying her was always in the cards, he would do it even more quickly now because of her pregnancy. Angela deserved more than 'baby mother' status.

Lola's death and the news of her pregnancy had brought them even closer than before. It was now as if they were truly one. Something had changed. He wasn't sure what it was, or if it was even tangible, but he could *feel* it.

His mobile rang, interrupting his thoughts. It was Tara. He ignored the call and without even giving it any thought, deleted her number. He then went through his phone and cleaned house.

By the time he was through he had deleted the contact information for forty-four women including Michelle, Elizabeth Rhoden, Cheetah, Patricia and Dimples. Even Laura got deleted. Some of the names he didn't even remember. He didn't know if that meant that he was no longer interested in anyone but Angela, but it felt right. His only focus right now was his wife to be, his unborn child, and his career.

He looked over at Gunner.

He was now awake.

Lenky's home was a hotbed of activity. The house was ripped apart and searched from top to bottom. The immediate neighbours watched in morbid fascination – nothing like this had ever happened in their affluent neighbourhood – through their hedges and windows as the cops moved back and forth, removing valuable items such as furniture, paintings and lots and lots of cash. Over twenty thousand US dollars, ten thousand pounds, and 4.5 million Jamaican dollars were found in a safe in Lenky's closet. Smaller quantities were found elsewhere in the house to which some of the cops helped themselves.

A black tinted Honda Ridgeline, which belonged to Lenky and was being driven by Cowboy, one of the gangsters in his inner circle that were supposed to meet with him at 11, drove by the house without stopping. Cowboy and the men inside the vehicle were shocked at the multitude of cop cars by the gate of Lenky's mansion. Even two vans belonging to the two rival local television stations were there. What the fuck had happened? For a second it had appeared that one of the cops was going to stop the truck but thankfully he hadn't. All four men aboard were armed to the teeth. There would've been a shoot out.

Cowboy didn't call Lenky's phone. He tried to reach a detective corporal that was on Lenky's payroll instead. The cop answered on the fourth ring.

"Yo, Barnes, ah Cowboy, mi just drive past Lenky yard and see a whole heap of police over deh. Yuh know what happen?"

"Rude boy yuh boss dead. Apprehension team from the States come down and storm the house today to extradite him back to America. Him engage them in a shootout and them buss him skull," the cop explained.

"Bumboclaat!" Cowboy exclaimed. He couldn't believe it. Just like that Lenky was gone. At least he had gone out like a soldier. A real gangster.

The cop told him that he was busy and had to go. Cowboy ended the call and told the men what he had just learnt. The men were shocked but expressed their admiration for the way Lenky had died with his gun in hand. They were proud of him.

Instead of turning back and having to go pass the house, Cowboy took a different route. He didn't want to chance being stopped by the cops. The men fell silent, each thinking about all the spoils that were there to be divided. Lenky owned lots of little unregistered businesses in various ghettoes that they could divide amongst themselves. Not to mention the stash houses that had guns and money. The organization was over. But life goes on. It was now up to every man to take what he could and forge his own his way.

The stash house that Cowboy was directly responsible for had over two hundred thousand dollars in cash, two uzis, a pump rifle and three desert eagles, a few ounces of cocaine and several pounds of marijuana. That was all his now. Including the truck that he was driving. He smiled inwardly at his good fortune.

"Yo, drive by 'im baby mother. We haffi give her the news an' mek she know say she nuh haffi worry herself. Ah whole heap ah money out deh fi Lenky. She haffi get some," Braveheart told Cowboy from his perch in the front passenger seat. Jada was his half-sister. He had to look out for her.

Cowboy wanted to tell him that the only man he took orders from was now dead but he chilled. It didn't make sense to get into it with Braveheart right now. Besides he was right. Jada was Lenky's original girl and the mother of his child. They had all liked her, she was cool and from the ghetto like them, unlike that bitch Lenky had gotten married to, who treated them with veiled contempt at best, like she was better than them.

Yeah, Jada deserved some money, for her and Lenky's son.

Just none of his.

"Hey mate," Gunner said groggily, rising and wincing. He had a massive headache. "Damn...I feel like shit."

"You look like it too," Jerome joked.

Gunner smiled weakly and flipped him the bird.

"Go take a shower and let's get you something to eat," Jerome suggested. "Oh and give me your ticket... I'll call the airline and reschedule your flight."

Gunner stood and yawned. He then retrieved the pouch in his hand luggage and took out the ticket. He handed it to Jerome and went inside the bathroom.

Jerome called the airline. He sweet-talked the attendant, who at first didn't believe that it was really Jerome James, and got her to bump someone from the flight that he would be leaving on in another eight days, so that he and Gunner would be able to travel together. He then called the front desk and asked them to send up a porter. Gunner was checking out of the hotel today. They would also need to go and see the owner of the rented SUV and pay him for another week.

The next major thing to deal with would be Lola's funeral. Her family needed to be contacted and arrangements had to be made. He would talk to Gunner about it later after he'd eaten and cleared his head a bit.

CHAPTER 37

When Cowboy pulled up in front of Jada's house, there were a lot of people outside her gate and in her yard, talking about what had happened. They fell silent when they saw the four gangsters who everyone knew were a part of Lenky's inner circle. A few people offered their condolences as the men walked by, stone faced.

The front door was locked. Cowboy banged on it. They could hear Jada screaming and crying inside, her pain piercing the humid afternoon air.

"Who that?" a shrill voice challenged.

"Cowboy. Open the door."

"Cowboy who?"

Cowboy struggled to control his temper. Who the fuck was this idiot who didn't know him? Obviously she wasn't from the neighbourhood. Everyone knew Lenky's inner circle.

"Hey gal open the fucking door and stop ask question!" he thundered.

The door flew open and they stepped in. Cowboy glared at the girl standing by the door. She had a piercing in her nose and at the side of her mouth.

Fucking freak, Cowboy mused. He wondered what her connection was to Jada. He had never seen her around here before. He felt like slapping the shit out of her for her insolence. Instead he walked over to where Jada was writhing on the carpet, alternating between whispering hoarsely and screaming. Two women, one of them her aunt, the other her neighbour, were trying to calm her down.

She was inconsolable.

The men went back outside and headed over to a small bar in the community that also doubled as a weed spot. Might as well make themselves comfortable.

They couldn't talk to Jada until she calmed down.

Laura woke up at 3 p.m. The medication had knocked her out. She had slept for five hours straight without stirring. She sat up, disoriented, not sure where she was. Then it all came back in a flood. Going to the clinic. No Jerome for support. The abortion. The pain. Khianna picking her up.

Groaning slightly, she got out of bed and went to the bathroom.

She could hear the television in the living room. Most likely Khianna was watching something fashion related. She thought about Lenky as she peed. He must have been trying to call her. She didn't even know where in the house she had left her phone. Her blood suddenly ran cold. It hit her like a ton of bricks. Suppose he had seen her phone and looked through it? Sweet Jesus. Fear like she had never known gripped her so tightly that her pain and discomfort were temporarily forgotten.

She flushed, wiped, and washed her face. She needed to get home and fast.

"I have to go Khianna," she said as she rushed out of the house. "I'll call you later and thanks for everything."

She shut the door behind her, not waiting for a response.

Khianna turned her attention back to the America's Next Top Model rerun.

She wondered what that was all about.

"Her father was a very important man in Cuba, before he fell out of favour with Castro," Gunner was saying, as he toyed with his bacon cheeseburger deluxe sandwich. He and Jerome were at the Metro Bar and Grill grabbing a bite to eat. "He feared for her safety and she was supposed to go to Florida, but time didn't permit. He had to quickly make arrangements to send her to Jamaica. A colleague of his had helped her get a job and get settled here. She had been here for eight months."

Gunner fell silent. A young couple entered the restaurant, holding hands. The guy said something to the girl and she giggled as they sat down a few tables away. Gunner, most of his face hidden behind over-sized Dior aviator shades, looked away and continued.

"She never heard from her family again. She feared the worst had happened...but had no way of finding out for sure."

"Damn, that's crazy," Jerome commented.

"Yeah...so other than the family friend there's no one to contact about her death..." Gunner's voice tailed off. He sighed deeply and took a sip of his soda.

"I still can't believe she's gone...they say its better to have loved and lost than never to have loved at all but I dunno...this is the hardest thing I've ever been through in my life," Gunner continued.

Jerome didn't want to say any of the typical death clichés like 'she's gone to a better place' or 'the good die young', so he remained quiet. Sometimes it was good enough to just listen.

"It's all my fault Jerome...she's dead because of me...I'll never forgive myself."

"Nah Gunner...don't think like that. Lenky's stupidity caused her death...and he will pay for his actions," Jerome said earnestly.

"I'm going to kill him Jerome," Gunner replied. "He cannot take my baby's life and live like its all good."

Jerome didn't argue with that. Gunner's tone was final.

"I'm going to call the guy later and let him know about Lola's death. His number is in her cell phone. I want it over with as soon as the cops release her body. I'm going to have her cremated Jerome...so I can always have her with me."

Jerome nodded solemnly.

CHAPTER 38

Laura's pulse raced when she arrived at her home. There were vehicles and people everywhere. She attempted to turn into the yard and a cop held up one hand, indicating for her to stop.

She did and put her window down.

"Officer, what the hell is going on here?" she demanded, her chest heaving with anxiety.

"And who are you?" the cop asked, his eyes taking in her full breasts, straining against her fitted red blouse.

"I'm Mrs. Bell and I live here. Now what the fuck is going on?"

"Don't curse at me lady, I'll arrest you for indecent language," the cop bristled.

Laura sucked her teeth, put the vehicle in park and hopped out.

"Come back here!" the cop commanded, as he strode towards her angrily.

Laura ignored him and walked up to a cop who seemed to be one of those in charge as he was standing there giving instructions.

The cop grabbed Laura on the shoulder from behind and she slapped his face.

"Hey!" the senior cop barked. "Constable, what are you doing?"

"Sir-" the constable began, stuttering in anger. He couldn't believe that the bitch had put her hands on him.

Laura walked up to the senior cop and introduced herself.

He appraised her coldly.

"Your husband is dead," he said bluntly. "He engaged the police in a shootout and was killed. Too bad, I'd rather have him locked up for the rest of his wasteful life. But he took the coward's way out. He basically committed suicide, he knew he couldn't have escaped."

Laura was stunned. Lenky was dead. Just like that.

"Luckily for you, you were not a subject of the investigation, so you're free to go. But you cannot go inside the house. It's a crime scene and everything has been confiscated. His bank accounts have also been frozen. All proceeds of criminal activity. I'm sure you'll be ok though...you'll just find another rich drug scum to marry," the cop sneered.

"Fuck you...you don't know anything about me," Laura retorted hotly. She couldn't believe that the cop was speaking to her like this.

"Sure I do...you pretty gold digging bitches are all the same. Now get the fuck out of here before an accident happens to you," he warned.

Laura recoiled and took an involuntary step back at the venom in the man's tone. She turned and fled, crying as she climbed into her truck and reversed out of the yard. Hundreds of articles of designer clothing and shoes, and thousands of dollars worth of jewellery, all gone.

She drove about two hundred meters away from the house and then pulled over on to the soft shoulder. She needed to clear her head for a second. Needed to think.

She was a widow. She would now have to take care of herself. The restaurant in New York was in her name along with Lenky's cousin as minority owner. It was doing well. His cousin surely wouldn't mind buying her out. She also had forty thousand dollars in her account at Sterling Bank in Manhattan. She would be ok. Lenky also owned a Brownstone in Queens that was in her name.

She had rented it out to a teacher and his family. She would give them notice as soon as she got back to New York. There was also some emergency cash at a location in Kingston that Lenky had told her about. She was the only one apart from him that knew that it was there. Yeah, she would be ok. The last two years had been good for the most part, and now she was free to move on with her life.

If only she had not had the abortion this morning. She would have been freely able to have Jerome's baby. Well, at least they were now free to be together. They could always have another child. She wondered if he had heard the news yet. She double checked to make sure that her social security card and her green card were in her pocketbook, then touched up her make-up and headed back to Khianna's apartment.

That's where she would stay until she got in touch with Jerome.

Then she would stay with him until it was time for him to go to England.

"Baby come quickly!" Angela said, waving her hand for emphasis, as Jerome opened the door. He ran over to her and looked at the TV. Lenky' s mug was on the right of the screen. Angela turned up the volume. Jerome sat down beside her and listened keenly as the attractive reporter recounted the biggest story of the day.

Jerome was stunned. He glanced at Gunner, who had walked in behind him. Gunner was staring at the TV, his eyes blazing with hatred. The reporter then moved on to the next story, a woman who was accidently shot and killed in a bizarre case of kinky sex gone awry.

"Damn..." Jerome muttered, still in shock. The last twenty four hours had been filled with enough drama to fill the pages of a novel. As far as he was concerned, justice was served. An innocent life had been lost because of Lenky. It was sweet karma that his life was snuffed out less than twenty four hours later.

Lenky had been a good friend to him when they had been cool, but he felt no sense of loss. Lenky deserved to die. He didn't respect life. He took it way too easily. And now his was gone. He wondered what was Lenky's final thought.

Angela walked over to Gunner and hugged him and kissed him on the cheek.

"Are you ok?" she asked softly.

Gunner gave her a sad smile.

"I'm not going to be *really* ok for a long time Angie. Life goes on. But it will never be the same."

Angela had no response for that.

Gunner sighed deeply.

Though it wouldn't bring Lola back, he was pleased that Lenky was dead.

He was just sorry that he wasn't the one who killed him.

CHAPTER 39

"Girl I just heard what happened over the news, I'm so sorry," Khianna gushed when Laura got back over there.

Laura sauntered inside and plopped down on the sofa.

"Would you believe the cops wouldn't even allow me to go inside the house? All my clothes, jewellery and stuff are confiscated. It's a wonder they didn't take my truck away from me," she vented.

"Wow, that's fucked up," Khianna commiserated, though she was surprised to hear no mention of the fact that Lenky was killed. Laura didn't seem perturbed in the least by her husband's death.

Laura is a cold fish, Khianna mused. *I wouldn't want to get on her wrong side.*

"Let me use your phone," she said to Khianna. She needed to go and pick up the money so that she could go shopping before the mall closed. All she had was the clothes on her back. But she needed to talk to Jerome now.

She was dying to tell him the good news.

Brownie told Calvin about Lenky's demise as soon as Calvin returned from his honeymoon. He had heard it on the news. Most of the community was in mourning. They had respected the gangster from Kingston that had been so good to Calvin and his wife. Calvin was stunned. His wife wasn't. She had dreamt last night that a huge gorilla, which was sitting on her husband, almost crushing him to death, suddenly got up and walked away. She had taken it to mean that a huge burden had been lifted. And she was right. Calvin no longer had the burden of being indebted to Lenky. He was free.

Calvin was sorry about Lenky's death.

Lenky had been good to him.

As he sat on the verandah with his wife and Brownie, he prayed for Lenky's soul to rest in peace.

"Did you hear about the murder of that young lady who had dinner here the other day?" Dahlia asked Sara. She was in Sara's room, sitting on the bed, watching Sara pack her things. Sara was going back to her apartment today.

Sara shook her head.

"Gunner's girlfriend?"

"Yes! She was shot and killed by someone who was trying to kill Gunner," Dahlia replied. "Such a shame. She was a very nice young lady. So pretty and polite. Angie said that Gunner is very distraught, as one can imagine."

"Wow, I'm really sorry to hear that," Sara said, as she zipped her suitcase shut. It was the second shooting death that she was hearing about today. Derrick had called earlier to tell her that his wife was dead. Apparently her cop boyfriend was giving her doggystyle while holding his gun to the back of her head and it went off, killing her instantly. So Derrick had gotten his divorce after all.

Sara shook her head. It was a crazy world. She lugged her suitcase out to the car. Her mother was behind her, still talking about the murder of Gunner's girlfriend. She was only half listening. What she really wanted to talk to her mother about was her complicit role in her husband's abuse of her. But it wasn't time. The wound had been freshly opened. She needed some more time before she could tackle that. And God help her mother when she did.

There was nothing that she could tell her that would justify her standing by idly while her husband sexually abused his youngest daughter.

Absolutely nothing.

That conversation would probably be the last they would ever have.

"Hey baby," Laura chirped, smiling into the phone.

"Who is this?" Jerome asked. He was sitting out by the community pool at Angela's apartment complex with Gunner, just chilling and talking about life. Angela was inside preparing dinner.

"This is Laura, Jerome," she replied, hurt that he didn't recognize her voice. "I still don't have my phone, I'm over by my friend's house. The one who came to pick me up...seeing as *you* couldn't be there."

"Are you ok?" Jerome asked, ignoring her last statement. If that was supposed to make him feel guilty it had failed miserably.

"Yeah...it was awful but I'm ok...baby, have you heard about Lenky?"

"Yeah, I heard." Jerome did not elaborate.

"Too bad I did the abortion this morning...turns out we could've had the baby after all."

Jerome didn't respond.

"Baby? You seem distant...what's up? You should be happy...we can be together now."

Jerome sighed. Might as well nip this in the bud and get it over with.

"Laura, we cannot be together. You know I have a girlfriend."

"But-"

"And I'm serious about her...matter of fact we can't see each other anymore."

"Jerome! What-"

"We had some good times L...and I liked you a lot... but things have changed. It's over," Jerome concluded.

Laura was too hurt and angry to speak. She couldn't believe what she was hearing. She thought that Jerome had loved her. The thought of not being in his life anymore overwhelmed her. The tears came fast and hard. She wailed into the phone. Khianna was watching Laura, listening in surprise to Laura's end of the conversation. She was positive that the Jerome in question was the football star.

So that's why Laura had been so upset that night at Mikey's wake when she saw Jerome with that singer. Khianna shook her head. You never saw smoke without fire.

Jerome started to say something and changed his mind. It didn't make any sense to prolong this. He knew that as long as he wasn't going to be with her, there was nothing that he'd be able to say to console her.

He hung up.

Several minutes passed before Laura realized that he had.

CHAPTER 40

Laura lit a cigarette as she turned the volume up on the TV. She had gone from being some- one who only smoked when extremely stressed out to almost a pack a day. It had been nine days since Jerome dropped her like a bad habit, and she had been smoking regularly ever since. She thought about him daily, alternating between hating and loving him each day. She wondered if she would ever really get over him.

She had booked a flight to New York the day after she had spoken to Jerome. She had gotten up early the next morning after crying her eyes out all night and went by the auto supplies store that Lenky secretly owned on Molynes Road. There was four hundred thousand dollars there in a safe in the small back office. The password had been easy to remember. It was her name.

She had given Khianna fifty thousand out of it, and used the balance to purchase an outfit to wear to New York, a one way ticket, and some US currency. She had left her truck with Khianna for it to be sold and the money wired to her account.

She was done with Jamaica. There was nothing there for her anymore but bad memories. She was staying with Steel until the tenants at her brownstone in Queens vacated the premises in another three weeks. Steel wanted to be her man but that wasn't going to happen. He satisfied her in bed but she needed more than that. Steel had his own business but he wasn't making the kind of money that she was used to. Being with him would be several steps down.

There was a cute drug dealer from Brooklyn that she met when leaving the hairdresser in Far Rockaway a few days ago. Money Making Mitch they called him. He was more her speed. She would see how that goes. He definitely stood a good chance if he played his cards right. She couldn't wait until she got her lump sum from Lenky's cousin for her share of the restaurant. He had agreed to buy her out and the paperwork and payment should be finalized in another week or so.

Her financial future was more or less secure. All she needed was a man to finance her lifestyle so that she wouldn't have to spend her money. She could hear the front door opening. Steel was home. She hoped that he didn't want any sex tonight. She was not in the mood. Besides, it was time to start keeping it tight for Mitch.

She chuckled at the thought.

Jada watched Nathaniel as he played a video game on his Xbox. She rubbed her stomach. He was going to get a little brother or sister, though she was positive that it was going to be a girl. She had finally gotten her wish, having another baby for Lenky, but he wouldn't be around to share in the joy. She missed him so much. Lenky could be a real asshole at times but he was her asshole. She had loved him since the day they met, when he was just an up and coming hustler, and she had loved him with all her heart ever since.

Not even when he had dissed her and got married to that bitch from New York did her love for him diminish in any way. She sighed deeply. At least she didn't have to worry about money. His kids would be well taken care of. Braveheart, bless his heart, had ensured that she got some money from all of Lenky's underground businesses. The money had totaled just over two million dollars. She knew that they kept a lot for themselves, but at least he had looked out for her.

The cops had finally released Lenky's body and his funeral was next week. She was going to ensure that he got a grand send off, no matter the cost. Lenky had lived like a king among men, and it was only fitting that he was laid to rest as such.

Karen felt sorry for Jada when she heard about Lenky's death, but it was not enough to make her go over there and make peace. She was no longer mad at her, but she didn't want to be friends with her again. With friends like Jada, who needed enemies?

She had gotten some closure. Hearing about the deaths of Ping Pong, and Blacka, who had succumbed to his injuries at the hospital, had helped to ease the pain. The fact that they were no longer alive made her feel better about the mental scars that they had left her with. One of them had given her a STD but thankfully it was one that was easily treated.

She had not had sex since the incident and her boyfriend had left her because she couldn't give him a reason why she didn't want to. She didn't blame him for walking away, as if the shoe was on the other foot she would have been angry and frustrated too, not knowing why he suddenly didn't want to have sex anymore.

But she just couldn't tell him about what had happened.

She hoped that with time, she would get over it enough to have a normal sex life again.

Sara sighed in contentment. She was lying on the couch in Derrick's arms, watching a movie. They were at her apartment. They alternated between both apartments, not really living together, but spending time with each other every day. With Renita dead, Derrick no longer had to worry about her contesting the divorce, and the house that he had left her with when he moved out was still his. He had put it on the market and the realtor had told him that there were six prospective buyers already. Sara had made it clear that she did not want to live there.

The plan was to elope and get married in six months. By then their properties would have been sold, and a home for the two of them bought. They had already identified a lovely four bedroom house in Barbican that would be perfect. They had spoken with the owner, a retired professor who was moving to Florida, and he had agreed to sell the house to them in principle.

She didn't know if she was going to work or be a stay at home mom as the plan was to have two children. She could decide that later. There was no rush. It certainly wouldn't be a decision based on finances as they would be well-off. With Derrick's growing practice and the money from her apartment, they would be quite comfortable financially.

Life was good.

And it was going to get even better.

Jerome and Angela were in the bedroom undressing. They had just gotten home from Jerome's send off dinner, courtesy of the Jamaica Football Association.

He was leaving to go to England tomorrow. He and Gunner were booked on the 11 a.m. flight. The invitation-only dinner was great, and well attended by many of Jamaica's prominent personalities. Gunner had attended, and was over by Jerome's apartment as he wanted to give the two of them some privacy on Jerome's last night. He was alone with Lola's ashes. The cremation had taken place six days ago and her ashes were in a custom made urn.

Aside from Gunner, they had yet to tell anyone about Angela's pregnancy.

"The dinner was really nice baby," Angela said as she took off her black Gucci pumps. She then removed her stockings and her black dress.

"Not as nice as desert," Jerome murmured, moving over to her. He was already nude, and his erection pressed against her stomach.

"Baby...mmmm..." Angela moaned as he kissed her deeply. She swooned in his arms.

He broke the kiss and positioned her on the chair next to the bed, spreading her legs wide, putting them on the arms of the chair.

He then got down on his knees and while he kissed the inside of her thighs, tantalizingly close to her quivering mound, he reached under the chair for the small black box that he had stashed there just before they went out.

Angela's eyes were partially closed and she moaned in anticipation of the feel of his tongue on her gaping sex.

Jerome removed the ring from the box.

He kissed her pussy softly. All over. Nibbled on her labia. Licked her folds. Stuck his tongue inside her wetness. Then he licked her clit. Fluidly. Back and forth. Held a steady rhythm. Angela gasped. She moaned. She felt like pulling her hair out. Her first orgasm of the night was on its way. It arrived. Angela convulsed and shuddered, flooding Jerome's welcome mouth with her juices.

"Baby, will you marry me?" Jerome said when he finally raised his head.

Angela thought that she heard him say something. She was still floating high above the clouds and was just slowly coming back down to earth.

"Mmmm...damn that was good. Did you say something baby?" She opened her eyes and they widened when she saw the ring in his hand.

"I did...I said, will you marry me?" Jerome was smiling, his mouth slick with her juices.

"Oh baby...you're so crazy...I love you so much...yes of course I'll marry you," Angela said, getting teary eyed.

Jerome slipped the ring onto her finger.

"It's beautiful baby," Angela said softly.

"Not as beautiful as you," Jerome responded before kissing her deeply.

Angela swore that she was going to burst with happiness.

Mrs. Angela Charlton-James.

Definitely had a nice ring to it.

EPILOGUE

Jerome hi-fived the player that he was replacing, Corluca, a forward from Croatia, and jogged on to the field to thunderous applause. It was thirty minutes into the first game of the season and the ardent Manchester FC fans were anxious to see how the highly touted Jamaican forward would fare in his debut. He was anxious too, not to see how he would do, as he knew that he would do well, but to get this new phase of his career underway. He planned to make an instant mark and either scoring or assisting on a goal or two would be the ideal way to announce that a new king was in town.

Angela, now two months pregnant, was seated in the VIP box, along with her parents and Gunner. They had arrived in England only yesterday, and were staying at the Radisson Edwardian hotel, located just fifteen minutes from the stadium. Sara had been invited but she declined. They had not laid eyes on her since she moved back to her apartment, and the only time any of them got to talk to her was when they called.

Angela had given up on reaching out, as she couldn't understand why Sara didn't want to have anything to do with the family. Dahlia still called Sara faithfully twice a week, enduring the cold, bland conversations that never lasted more than a few minutes.

David couldn't care less.

They soaked in the eclectic atmosphere, watching Jerome's every move on the pitch. He was already making his presence felt, and had dazzled the crowd on two occasions with his skillful dribbling and slick passing. Angela gasped when Jerome was brought down from behind by a nasty tackle from the Birmingham left back. Jerome was slow to get up, and had to be helped up by two of his teammates.

He shook off the effects of the tackle and made his way into the eighteen yard box. The free kick sailed in and Jerome rose high between two defenders and headed the ball beyond the hands of the airborne goalkeeper and into the right hand corner of the net. The stadium, filled to capacity with sixty-six thousand fans, erupted.

Jerome, not caring about the yellow card that he would get for the act, pulled off his jersey and ran to the side of the field where the VIP box was located in the stands. He managed to celebrate with a little dance move before he was mobbed by his teammates.

"Yeah! I love you baby!" Angela shouted, though she knew that he couldn't hear her.

Gunner applauded and grinned. Jerome had kept his promise after only being on the pitch for twenty-two minutes.

He had scored his first goal in the English Premier League.

And it was dedicated to Lola.